DULU

BY MATT PETERSON

ILLUSTRATIONS BY: JACOB DANIELS

DULU
by Matt Peterson
illustrated by Jacob Daniels, Overflowstudios.org
Copyright, 2016

ISBN: 978-1537690988
Cover Illustration: Jacob Daniels
Cover Design: Lauren Olinger
Layout: Dana Zondory, dzondory@aol.com

Website: Dulukids.com
Contact: RedCardinalStudio.com

FOR MORE INFORMATION OR TO ORDER PRINTS, VISIT DULUKIDS.COM

DEDICATED:

To my beautiful wife, DEBBIE, for her patience, love, encouragement, and selflessness as she has served, taught, trained, enjoyed, and educated our five young men. This book is also dedicated to our remarkable sons: JOSIAH, SETH, SAM, JOHN and ANDREW for drawing out bedtime stories when they were young, living large, and embracing the adventure they were placed on earth to live. You are loved and *nothing is impossible*.

TABLE OF CONTENTS

INTRODUCTION

This allegory is a story of adventure, of danger, of power, and battles with unseen evil. This is also a story about the discovery of love and warmth, of healing and new songs that have never been sung before. This is a story about kids similar to you who, out of hurt and curiosity, began a quest that ended up changing their lives and the lives of many. This story begins in a special but darkened place—a place called Dulu.

Chapter One

THE ROCK

Even from a great distance the Dulusians could see it. Rising high into the sky over the land of sand stood the mysterious and majestic Magnifikiyah. Magnifikiyah, or "Nifi" as most people called it, was the only mountain in Dulu, and it was so tall that the top was often cloaked in fluffy clouds. Aisha quietly stared at the mountain, visible through the clouds on this day, her heartbeat increasing, one hand tightly gripping her school bag handle. She had been headed to school, but a morning peal of thunder from the mountain shook the ground, freezing her feet in place for a moment.

11

Aisha often felt frightened when looking at the ominous mountain, which would send a tingle down her spine. At other times, she felt peace when looking up at the Nifi. On this day, while Aisha stared at the lonely mountain, she felt longing—a longing inside of her for something more than what she had or knew. Somehow Aisha knew that Magnifikiyah was holding secrets. Behind the fear and power the mountain exuded, Aisha believed there were mysteries to discover from Nifi—maybe even the mysteries of why she was born and why there was sadness in Dulu. She wished that the mountain would tell her what it knew and not just stand there making everyone afraid.

Magnifikiyah (which means "the Ancient One") was a lonely mountain because it was the only place in Dulu that the people were unable to visit. Between Aisha and the massive mountain was a breath-taking and bottomless crevasse in the sand. The wide chasm encircled Nifi entirely, like a gigantic black snake, separating the great mountain from every person in Dulu. This crevasse was known as the "death pit" because everything that fell into it was gone forever, disappearing into the darkness. Over the centuries, many people had tried to construct bridges large enough to cross over the death pit from the desert of Dulu to reach the feet of Nifi—but every bridge had failed, and many people had lost their own lives trying. Anyone who came near the pit felt a sense of evil lurking below and smelled the foul stench of the netherworld rising to the surface. No one knew what type of monstrous creatures might live in the black pit, perhaps feasting on those who fell in. Most Dulusians stayed far away from the chasm. So the lonely mountain stood silent, alone.

If a person in Dulu were to step out of his home early in the morning and listen ever so patiently, he might hear the winds sing. Voices were often heard singing songs in the wind that moved swiftly down Nifi's long ridges each morning, flowing all the way down across the death pit and onto the desert sands of Dulu far below. The people of Dulu called these morning winds "mercy winds." A few in Dulu woke up early enough to rise, dress and venture outside to hear the wind songs as the sun rises out of its night cave, but most people missed them while getting ready for school or sleeping comfortably in their beds.

Dulu

A few very old men in the land still spoke of ancient legends. They told stories from thousands of years ago when the death pit did not exist and the ancestors of Dulu actually lived on Nifi. These legends described Dulusians eating enormous fruit and living among a variety of strange creatures that spoke to people and roamed the land in those days. The old men said that the ancestors of Dulu would climb all the way to the top of Magnifikiyah and fly upon the backs of large eagles. Some described them even riding upon fish that swam in cool rivers. Old books about the mountain spoke of a living kind of water that flowed down Nifi's side, causing all who drank of it to never thirst again. It also said that there were lush meadows and gigantic trees that seemed to touch the sky—trees with large limbs that moved to music and clapped to singing. These are only legends of course, legends that seemed hard to imagine in Dulu, especially since the pit had devoured all of the dreamers, swallowing the hopes of living on the mountain again. Years without dreams made old legends fade, and the old books were forgotten and viewed as fairy tales.

The Rock

Fortunately for Dulu, dreams and stories were not entirely a thing of the past. On one crisp and starry desert night, an especially strange thing happened while most in Dulu were sleeping. The mountain that had stood mostly quiet for thousands of years, the mountain that Aisha had stared at earlier in the day and had wished would speak and reveal mysteries, suddenly began shaking and quaking violently as if it were trying to say something of utmost importance. Aisha woke up, shaken out of her dreams, and sat up in her bed. She felt the shaking from the mountain through the floor and heard its rumbling. She glanced out her window into the darkness toward the mountain but could see nothing. She then swung her bare feet out from underneath the warm covers onto the stone floor and stepped toward the window in her small room. She opened the window and felt a burst of cool breeze blow onto her face. Then everything was completely still, calm and peaceful. Aisha felt like something important was about to happen in the still night. Maybe the mountain was about to begin answering questions. Just as she had that thought, a shooting star flashed brightly above the mountain and shot across the sky, illuminating the whole of Dulu for a second. She may have been the only one to see the brilliant fire that divided the darkness up above.

What Aisha didn't know as she stared at the mountain and the light flash was that something was happening, the kind of happening that had never been before, nor would ever take place again. When the rumble and shaking was heard through all the land of Dulu, a large portion of the mountain broke loose near the top of Nifi. This Rock had been a part of Nifi before Dulu existed, before the death pit had appeared. The big Rock that had been a part of the face of the Ancient One before time began was now dispatched toward Dulu.

In the darkness, the dislodged stone began descending. It crushed, crashed, smashed and tumbled down the mountainside. As it rolled from the great heights of Nifi toward Dulu, portions of the large Rock flew off. Jagged edges became rounded and beautiful layers of ancient stone shot away like missiles. The massive stone was changing appearance with its tumbling decent from the very top of the world as it traveled toward the death pit. As it rolled, it diminished in size, loosing elements of beauty and power with every spin.

The Rock

Down through meadows at dizzying speed, dashing over small trees and down the long ridges of Nifi in the darkness, the Rock raced toward the pit at bullet speed. Then, only a moment before it flew into the death pit, it hit a large bump that launched the rounded stone far into the air and over the huge chasm, clearing it entirely!

The Rock touched down safely on the ground on the other side, speeding through the sand until it finally came to rest in valley of Dulu far below. What had been the highest and most beautiful of all rocks during every age of Dulu was suddenly gone from its place and changed, lying alone in the desert sand miles below.

Some people of Dulu were awakened by the quaking of the mountain and echoes from the rolling Rock, but most in Dulu just kept sleeping and snoring.

Not far from the pit, a handful of shepherds had been drinking, laughing and telling stories around a campfire that crackled and danced into the night air. Their sheep quietly rested near them. When the shepherds heard the shaking and rumbling of the mountain, they stopped talking and stood still, becoming very afraid as they heard something coming closer. Suddenly, the Rock shot past them like a bullet. The speed at which the Rock whipped by caused a wind to follow, blowing off their hats and knocking them to the ground. The astonished men tried to understand what had happened. A moment later, they sprang to their feet, re-lit their lamps and ran after the unknown object. Following its trail in the sand under the clear night sky, the men came near their village and discovered the Rock's now motionless form lying peacefully in the sand. The Rock seemed like a meteor from another world. They approached it carefully, warily.

Some of the men wondered if it was hot or if it would explode as they peered upon the weird stone through dancing shadows of lantern light. They carefully examined the Rock under their flickering light, touching it gently and jabbing it with sticks. They finally arrived at the conclusion that it wasn't dangerous. In a few short minutes, fear turned to joy, and the men began singing and doing the Dulu dance around the foreign object, telling each other how great and wonderful the gift from Nifi was. Perhaps the men had a little too much Dulu juice to drink, or perhaps they simply loved having a piece of Nifi in Dulu that they could see and touch. On this special night, the Rock reminded them of the mountain everyone in Dulu could see when they looked up—Magnifikiyah.

"Tomorrow, let's tell the people about the Rock that Nifi has sent to us," they said, and they happily went back toward their sheep, singing and laughing along the way at their near-death experience.

The following day, some of the people who came to see the Rock made fun of it because it didn't look like Nifi at all, and they thought that the men who told them about it were a bit crazy. In the morning light, the Rock was plain, had no sparkling diamonds or rubies and was brown in color, just like the towels that everyone used to wipe the sand off of their feet. The Rock didn't flash with light, glow or do anything else special. The people didn't believe that the Rock came from the Ancient One because it didn't look beautiful or strong, and it surely didn't look like Nifi. And everyone in Dulu knew that it was impossible to cross the death pit.

"Nothing has ever crossed the death pit before," some began saying to one another.

Dulu

"This Rock is a fake—it didn't come from Nifi," others voiced.

Many agreed and turned back to their homes, not interested and not believing that the Rock came from Nifi. What was a wonder to the shepherds was only a misfit stone to nearly everyone else. A few of the simple people in Dulu liked having such a large and quiet Rock in the land of sand, but most people quickly forgot that the Rock was even there.

Many days after the Rock arrived, young Aisha was slogging through the sand as fast as she could, her bag flopping and her hair disheveled as she ran. She took quick glances behind her to see if they were coming. Aisha was a little shorter than others her age, with dark hair, beautiful dark brown eyes and browned skin. She was once again running away from the Brock boys, who enjoyed picking on her. They had pulled her hair and made mean comments to her when she was on her way home from school. "The Brock Twins," as they were called by all of the community kids, were about two years older than Aisha and seemed to enjoy being jerks, always picking on the younger kids. After saying some hurtful things to her about her size and then yanking her hair, they let her run away. Aisha ran

20

awhile and hid behind the Rock that was lying in the sand. She sat down behind it and began to cry, frustrated more than anything.

"I hate those boys!" Aisha said angrily, slapping the Rock as she sobbed, wishing she had a big brother to protect her and imagining how he would give both of the twins a punch.

Between her sniffles and imagining a big brother, Aisha thought she heard someone say something. She stopped crying and listened, afraid that they were looking for her.

"Aisha," she heard very softly, like a whisper. Aisha quickly looked around to see who it was, ready to run again from the Brock boys, but there was no one there. She was alone with the Rock.

Then again she heard the voice: "Aisha." The voice seemed to be coming somehow from the Rock itself. It was a familiar voice, kind of like her dad's voice or her Uncle Dave's voice. She didn't know who it was, but it made her heart feel like a friend was calling her.

Standing up and staring at the Rock in the sand, Aisha whispered through her tears, "Who is

Dulu

messing with me? Rocks don't talk." She reached out and felt the hard surface of the stone.

Just as she spoke, she heard him speak again. "I want to help you."

Pausing for a moment and then looking around, she replied, "Who are you, and where are you?"

"Climb up and stand on top of me and you'll see how I can help you," promised the voice. "Go ahead. There is a hole in my side that you can place your foot in and climb up," He nudged.

Aisha had never been on top of a rock and had certainly never talked to a rock. She thought that she was just making up these words in her mind, but right before her eyes was a hole big enough for a child's foot to fit into. She looked around to see if anyone was watching and then carefully raised her leg as high as she could to place her foot in the hole and began climbing up the Rock. Reaching the top and now standing on the Rock, she realized that she wasn't sad anymore. Even stranger, she suddenly felt fresh and clean inside. She then thought to herself something that she normally doesn't think: *Who cares if the kids call me names. Why should I feel sorry for myself, no matter*

REACHING THE TOP AND NOW STANDING ON THE ROCK,
SHE REALIZED THAT SHE WASN'T SAD ANYMORE.

what others do? The words were similar to what her Dad would say to her.

"You are safe," the voice then said, "and you are not crying anymore." Aisha touched her face with her hands to feel the tears. Her tears were gone.

The tune of a song her mom sometimes sang came to Aisha's mind. She began to hum quietly as she viewed the village and noticed how the birds were chirping loudly and cheerfully, flying in the deep blue sky above her head.

Just as Aisha began to enjoy standing on top of the Rock, another unusual thing began to happen. The talking Rock began to grow. For a few seconds, it magically grew larger in every direction under her feet, and then it stopped suddenly with a trembling under her feet. Aisha steadied herself and regained her balance, now knowing for sure that the Rock was alive. She nervously danced around with chills traveling up her spine. To her, the Rock seemed to have grown to be as large as her house!

"What is happening? How did you get bigger like that?" asked Aisha, a little frightened and amazed at this magic Rock.

The Rock

"Aisha, you don't need to be afraid," she heard quietly. "I just grew a little larger, but you have become a little smaller, too," replied the Rock. "Each time people hear my voice and do what I ask, I begin to get larger, and they begin to get smaller."

Aisha looked down at her hands and feet. They didn't look or feel any smaller, but the Rock certainly looked bigger than it did before.

Aisha could hear the words from the Rock, but she couldn't find a nose or eyes or see the mouth that was speaking. "How can you talk to me when you are only a Rock?" asked Aisha curiously, looking around carefully to find where the sound was coming from.

"I speak from the inside of me, to the inside of you," said the Rock. "You can only hear me if you listen; but I am always here to talk and to be climbed upon whenever you need me."

"What is your name? And how did you know my name?" Aisha asked, beginning to believe.

"I have a lot of names, but why don't you just call me the Rock for now," He said calmly. "I've known you for a very long time. But it is just today that you have begun to hear and know me," He said.

Dulu

Looking around Dulu from on top of the Rock, Aisha noticed the round, short, adobe-looking homes in the village and the prickly dardruk trees interspersed throughout the sand. Her eyes were drawn to the Dulusians mulling around aimlessly. As she watched them carefully, she began to feel sad again, but in a different way than when the twins were troubling her. It seemed that people were looking for something to make them happy, but they were aimless and looked hopeless. Aisha saw a woman arguing with another woman from one side of the Rock. Then she noticed a young boy with crutches, struggling through the deep sand on the other side of the Rock.

"Why do the people look so sad?" whispered Aisha, as she watched an older man shuffling past, his head bowed low.

"The people look sad because everyone in Dulu needs freedom and purpose, but they don't know how to find them," He said.

"I want to help them," replied Aisha, feeling a new sense of compassion inside of her. "How can I help them feel like I feel right now?" she asked.

"You can help them by doing what I have done. I came down from the top of Nifi to help you, and now you must climb down from me to help them," He said encouragingly.

"You really came from Nifi?" Aisha questioned excitedly, hoping it was true. She remembered staring at the mountain and hoping for answers.

"Yes," the Rock spoke emphatically. Aisha looked up at the distant mountain and tried to figure out how the Rock came to Dulu. "I am a part of the secret that you hoped to find. I am the mystery that came down to you," He said.

Aisha remembered staring at the mountain many times and having that inner knowing that it held secrets.

"I don't want to leave... I love it here," said Aisha. "I'd like to stay longer."

"It is time to begin," said the Rock. "How would you like to begin the greatest adventure anyone has ever been on?" He invited and waited.

Aisha could only think of stories of adventure she had read in books or stories that her Dad had told her. *What kind of adventure could the Rock possibly offer, since he was stuck in sand and missing legs?* She questioned internally, picturing herself on a hike through the desert with a picnic lunch by herself.

Dulu

"An adventure beyond what you can imagine," the Rock replied to her thoughts. "One that will change your life and the lives of many others."

The word "okay" slipped out of Aisha, even though she had no idea what an immovable stone possibly had to offer. She just felt that it was right and somehow this was a good thing. Besides, he was a talking Rock. Perhaps he could do more than talk.

"Wherever you go, I'll be with you," the Rock then said to her. "You will hear my voice just as you do now. You just won't see me."

With that, Aisha felt enough courage to climb down from the Rock. As she stood in the sand, the Rock said, "Before you go, pick up a handful of sand and count all of the small grains for me." Aisha bent down and grabbed a handful of sand. As she began counting, sand fell through all of her fingers to the ground, and she realized that there were far too many grains of sand in her hand to count even a fraction of them.

"Whoops," Aisha said out loud, as the sand fell through her fingers. "I cannot count all of them—it's impossible."

The Rock

"I think about you a lot, Aisha," the Rock said genuinely. Aisha looked up from the falling sand at the motionless stone.

"Each grain of sand in the land of Dulu represents a thought that I have for you. You can never count them all, but wherever you go, I'll always be thinking of you. When you are sleeping and when you are awake, when you are happy and when you are lonely, remember that I'm thinking about you."

When the Rock said that, Aisha felt a rush of love like she had never felt in her life. Her heart was flooded with warmth as if large hands were holding it. Aisha knew that her mom and dad loved her very much, but this love was different and even more powerful. A smile appeared on Aisha's face, and she looked in wonder at the plain-looking Rock and then up at the mountain that he came from. It didn't seem possible; it felt like a dream come true somehow, and like she was the single most important person in Dulu.

"With all of the sand in Dulu, I must be loved more than anyone else in the world," she sincerely thought to herself, believing that the Rock was telling the truth. Aisha again looked at the people walking around and had a sense that she could do anything because she was loved so much.

Aisha picked up her book bag, turned and ran toward home to tell her parents about the Rock. Looking back at him once more, she felt like it was a brand new day and she was a brand new person—a person with a new friend.

Running upon the sand seemed much easier than it ever had before. Instead of causing her feet to sink down, the sand now helped lift her every step and carry her home. *Every step, He thinks about me*, Aisha thought to herself along the way.

Flinging open the front door and out of breath, Aisha quickly brushed some of the sand off of her feet with the brown towel hanging outside and talked rapidly to her mom who was standing in the kitchen, preparing a meal. She quickly told her about the Brock Twins and excitedly mentioned the voice that she had heard. She even told her about how the Rock grew and the reason for sand in Dulu. While Aisha spoke, her mom turned and listened to every word and smiled with a slightly puzzled look on her face. When her story was finished, her mom said, "Wow, you have had a quite a day, Aisha," looking back down at the food she was

THE ROCK

cutting up. "You probably need to tell your father about this at dinner," she said as she leaned over and kissed her on the forehead. Looking at her with a sparkle in her eyes, her mom said, "Now it's time to eat, honey. Why don't you go get washed up and call your dad."

Aisha thought her mom would be more excited about the Rock. *But that's okay*, she thought to herself. *I'll tell her more tomorrow and take her there to see it herself.*

At dinner Aisha told her dad about the Rock and he had a similar response. He smiled and was kind, but he certainly didn't believe yet. When Aisha went to bed that night, she gazed out her open window at the flashes around the top of Nifi on the distant horizon, lighting up his stone face. She grinned and pulled the blanket up under her chin. She began thinking about how the Rock was once up there in the flashes, and now he was here in the sand. The great mountain held secrets after all, and she had just learned one of them.

The next morning, the first sunbeams of the day shined on Aisha's face, and the mercy winds blew gently through her bedroom window, waking her up. When she opened her eyes, she remembered the Rock again and wished that she was with him, wondering for a moment if he was real or if she had dreamed him up during the night.

Then, very softly, like a friend whispering her name, his calm internal voice came to her again: "Good morning Aisha."

The Beginning.

Chapter Two

THE DOOR

Aisha ran into her parents' bedroom and woke them up like it was Christmas morning, begging them to come see the Rock with her. They rubbed their eyes, hesitated, and then they yawned widely and finally decided to join her. They sat up in bed slowly, hair pointing in all different directions, and put on their slippers. Aisha bounced down the small stairway to the bottom floor and out the front door, still in her pink and yellow pajamas. The mercy winds were swirling around Dulu, removing the tiredness and thoughts of their warm beds, as Aisha tugged on her parents' hands and pulled them across the sand toward

33

the Rock. The adults glanced at one another and smiled as Aisha led the way. All of them looked a bit silly with their pajamas and wild hair. Aisha's father had heard about the Rock from a man at his work named Gil, but he hadn't said anything to Aisha. Gil was a friendly man in his forties. He had a bushy brown beard, extraordinarily large eyes and a protruding belly that flopped over his belt and jiggled up and down when he laughed at his own jokes—which happened a lot. Gil had never been married, and he was a bit loud, never afraid to tell anyone what was on his mind. Gil was also known for enjoying too many pubba sticks. (Pubbas are animals that look something like a pig and a rabbit mixed together. When pubbas are cooked, they put the chunks of meat on a stick covered in lots of thick, sweet and tasty sauce.) Gil had seen the Rock himself, but he wasn't too impressed. He told Aisha's father matter-of-factly that it was "just like a big piece of sand.nothing at all to look at." As the three approached the Rock, Aisha let go of her parents' hands and ran to it. Her parents followed and then stood looking at one another, then the Rock, then one another again, neither one knowing quite what to say or think. In their loss of words, Aisha filled in the gap, excitedly pointing to the hole in his side, telling them all over again how she had cried and showing them where she had hid. As Aisha recounted every detail, her Mom reached out to touch the Rock and feel its surface in a gesture of kindness, like someone patting the head of a stray dog. As she touched the Rock's rough surface, a surge of warmth went into her hand, up her arm, through her elbow, then down through her body, warming her right knee. She stepped back from the Rock quickly, as if slightly shocked by electricity, and she realized she felt no pain in her knee for the first time since she had hurt it working in the garden two years earlier. She bent it back and forth, very surprised at the missing pain. "Mom! I told you He was alive. The Rock fixed your knee!" Aisha joyfully exclaimed while her father just watched in silence.Her mom kept rubbing her knee, puzzled and unsure of what had just taken place. Aisha's dad seemed to be staring off into the distance with the same look on his face that he sometimes had when he was thinking of his work, not really paying attention to what had just happened to her mom.

After a short while, Aisha's dad decided it was time to head back home before any of the neighbors got out of bed and saw them in their pajamas.

"Hey Aisha," he said with an unexpected sound of surprise, "how about we race home and you can help me make some of our special cannah cakes for breakfast this morning?" Aisha wanted to stay longer, but she knew her parents weren't quite as excited about the Rock as she was. "Okay," she said with a half-smile, a bit disappointed.

On the way back, Aisha asked her parents if they had heard the Rock speak to them. They said no, but Aisha's dad tried to make her feel better. "It sure is a nice rock, sweetie. It's very nice to have a rock like that in Dulu, and it was a perfect morning for a walk in the mercy winds. We should do this together more often," he said with a glance at his wife and a small grin.

Although disappointed that they didn't hear the Rock speak, Aisha began thinking about the friends she wanted to tell about the Rock when they reached home. It was Saturday morning, which meant no school and only fun today.

The Door

After breakfast, Aisha quickly grabbed the phone and began calling her friends, starting, of course, with her best friend, Isabelle. Isabelle had reddish hair and lots of freckles. She was only one week older than Aisha, and they both loved sandball and Dulu dancing. Isabelle was a tomboy who was strong enough to beat up most of the boys her age and a very good athlete.

Aisha also called Lucas and Missy, a brother and sister who lived next door. Lucas was twelve, the oldest, tallest and most responsible of all her friends. Missy was sweet, inquisitive and everyone's friend. Then she called her younger cousin, Rolly. Rolly was very kind and quiet. He was extremely smart but lacked confidence, physical size and strength. He was the kind of kid who would often get overlooked or picked last for games. Last on her short list of friends was Kaboo, who was a lot of fun to be with but also tended to get into mischief at times. Kaboo loved adventure, would try nearly anything and was always coming up with new games to play and things to do.

She told them she had a surprise to show them, and they all agreed to meet at Aisha's house in an hour. An hour later, the kids began showing up—except for Kaboo. He was late as usual, but he finally arrived with the remains of some kind of bright red dessert around his mouth. Aisha and her five friends set out to see the Rock. The always-curious Isabelle kept asking Aisha about the surprise. Aisha refused to tell her anything and just kept saying, "You'll see," with a grin. Dulu was so boring that no one expected much of a real surprise anyway.

These six very different friends always seemed to enjoy doing things together. Lucas loved justice, always tried to do the right thing and sometimes tended to police the rest of the kids as first-borns sometimes do. As he walked behind Aisha and Isabelle, who were busily talking, he tried to imagine where they were going and wished they would pick up the pace. Sweet Missy and little Rolly followed behind Lucas. They were more on the shy side, the youngest of the group. They talked about a TV show they had both watched the night before about a group of kids competing in desert games to win a large sum of money. Although shy around everyone else, they seemed to enjoy talking to one another, as Rolly explained how the blue team on the show could have performed better while using a commonly known scientific approach. Missy agreed, though she didn't understand what he was talking about. All the while, Kaboo was zig-zagging his way through them, carving designs with his shoes in the deep sand, completely unaware of anything else going on around him.

When the crew of kids arrived at their destination, the boys were unexpectedly happy to find the large Rock to ascend. Kaboo quickly climbed on top of the strange-looking stone, and Lucas and Rolly followed him. Missy and Isabelle listened as Aisha told them about the voice she heard the day before. After several jumps off the stone like paratroopers jumping out of a plane, little Rolly became distracted by something. Rolly knelt down on top of the Rock and began muttering something to himself that sounded like "I'm sorry," and looking as if he had a great weight bearing down upon his shoulders. His little head was bowed, and he appeared dejected. It was as if he was all by himself, and the rest of the kids, after noticing him, silently paused from their stories and free-falling with curiosity and concern.

"Hey, what's wrong with Rolly?" Missy asked the girls.

A few moments into the still silence, Rolly whispered, "Yes, I will," quietly yet confidently. He paused another moment while pondering his decision, and then the weight looked like it lifted from his shoulders. Looking up as if newly transported back to Dulu, he saw everyone staring at him with silent concern. Rolly's face seemed to glow a golden color, and a smile flashed across his face from ear to ear. He was not embarrassed at all by his tears. His shoulders straightened, and he stood to his feet. A boldness rose within him, and he began talking out loud to Dulu like he had words that the land needed to hear him say. Little Rolly seemed a bit taller as he began speaking: "The time is coming when your chains will be broken!" He then pointed at the land and the village and shouted, "You will soon be changed and called Lutru!"

His friends were shocked. They looked at one another with proud yet awe-struck smiles, and then Kaboo let out a laugh at the sight of his small friend shouting at the village. Somehow Rolly's personality had changed in a moment; he was transformed into someone strong and bold.

After a short laugh, Kaboo joined in, yelling to Dulu at the top of his voice. Lucas followed, shouting, "Yaaaaaah, Dulu!" All three boys began jumping off of the Rock again like they were now superheroes jumping down to save the world.

Aisha paused for a moment, silently pondering what "Lutru" was and what must have just happened to her young cousin. She continued telling her story to the girls as the boys raced up the Rock and jumped off again, over and over. Aisha then came to the point in her story where she bent down and picked up a handful of sand. Holding the sand, she told them that each grain represented a thought the Rock had for each of them. With these words, Isabelle felt a sudden rush of cool wind across her chest and into her heart. She could feel the love that Aisha spoke of, and she became aware that the Rock behind her was alive—eerily alive. She slowly turned around and took a step toward Him, placing both hands on Him, putting her ear upon Him.

In the midst of the noise from the boys' yelling, Isabelle suddenly heard his voice as clear as her own father's voice on her inside, and she saw an animated vision in her mind like watching a movie at the theater. She closed her eyes and saw herself running through the midst of thousands of wandering people. They were old and young, of all colors, shapes and sizes, all looking in a different direction for something they could not see. She pressed through them toward a light that shined in the distance. All of a sudden, powerful creatures like giant lions with broad wings swooped from the sky near to her and then looked to the light behind them. Very quickly, the people and then the creatures turned and disappeared. She found herself alone, standing before massive steps and the most beautiful man she had ever seen, who was seated at the top. He had flowing white hair and looked as strong as any man she had ever seen, and she knew that He was very wise.

The man was staring at her with eyes full of love and compassion, looking at her as her father did. He invited her to come closer, and one glance told her she could not be safer with any man. She climbed up the stairs, fell into His arms and began feeling a warm wind blowing through her insides, cleansing and touching all of her heart.

As tears of comfort and wholeness streamed down her face, she began to feel larger tears dripping on top of her head from the father-like person who was embracing her. She reached up to touch her wet hair and heard Aisha's voice saying, "Let's go home Isabelle. It's starting to rain." With her eyes still closed, the vision stopped. She could smell the strong, fresh fragrance of rain in the air and the drops on her face. Isabelle slowly pushed herself away from the Rock while the warm rain began pouring down upon their heads and a soft roll of thunder echoed in the distance. Isabelle looked up and smiled. She felt at peace, loved and clean.

Running through the sand and the puddles, the six friends began singing their favorite Dulu rain song called "Washed Away" as they splashed their way home. The words of the song told of a rain that takes all pain away, soft rains from the Ancient One, cleansing the land and bringing fun. Rolly playfully threw water from a puddle into the air, and he seemed older, more joyful and free than he had ever been before.

Arriving at their homes, the six soaked friends agreed to meet at the Rock the next morning—with their parent's permission, of course.

Later that night, now dry and in bed once again, Aisha lay thinking about the Rock and the day full of wonder. Thunder continued to roll in the night sky, and flashes of lightening lit up her room, casting shadows on the opposite wall. She quietly asked, "Are you still there?" She hoped He would still respond, though she hadn't heard Him speak since the morning. Quietly, His soft, warm voice answered, "I am with you always, Aisha, even to the end of time. I'll never leave you. Sleep well."

Very early the next morning, the six set out for the Rock that rested on the outskirts of Dulu. The rains from the day before had continued through the afternoon and late into the night, with the thunder having kept most of them up late, snuggling with their pets or crawling into bed with their parents. A warm foggy mist arose from the sands of Dulu as they walked toward the Rock through the quiet, thick air.

Along the way, instead of carving through the sand, Kaboo stayed with the group and wanted to say something.

"I had a weird dream last night guys," he said as the others listened and walked. "I've never had a dream like this before. I saw a huge superhero guy that flew through the sky with some kind of electric clothes on. This guy was stronger than even Superman, and light came off of his weird-looking suit." Kaboo then pointed toward the top of Nifi that was just poking up above the fog. He moved his arm across the sky while describing his dream: "Then he flew over Nifi like a shooting star and zoomed down into the death pit, lighting the whole thing up!"

"What!?" Isabelle said with a laugh, wondering, with everyone else, if he was joking.

The look on Kaboo's face seemed sincere.

"For real. It was a weird dream, but it seemed so real and cool," Kaboo said and started walking again, unsure if they believed him.

"Then, the flying guy—Light-Man or something, came up out of the pit carrying a big door in his arms, and that was all," Kaboo finished.

"Wow!" said Aisha. "Did anything else happen?" she inquired.

"Nope," Kaboo said, continuing to walk with hands in his pockets.

The children did not know what to make of the dream, and it was pretty odd that it was about someone coming out of the death pit with a door in his hands, but it was still very cool. Every kid loves superheroes, and none of them had ever had a dream about one before.

They began walking through the fog until they came to the place where the Rock had been the day before—or where Aisha thought it had been before. Aisha started pacing around in the thin mist, walking over toward a dardruk tree that she knew was near the Rock. Maybe they were in the wrong place, or perhaps the fog had led them astray. Aisha looked at the dardruk tree closely and saw the "DP" initials that someone had carved in it years ago. It was the right tree. She ran back over to where the Rock should be, and there was nothing. Everyone began looking all around for the Rock, searching with a sense of urgency. Aisha and her friends spread out and combed the area while the mist thinned and began to lift. Glancing down on the ground, Lucas knelt down and noticed that the sand was pressed with the image of the Rock that was once there. The kids ran over and looked at the depression in the sand, and a chill ran up their spines. Something didn't feel right.

"What is going on here?" Lucas questioned out loud, all of them mystified at what could have happened.

Then Kaboo noticed a trail from one side of the depression in the sand.

"Someone dragged it away!" cried Kaboo.

"And it's headed toward toward the death pit!" Isabelle shouted, as a strange fear fell upon them. Kaboo looked wide-eyed for a moment and then ran quickly along the trail, the five others close behind him. The sand revealed many footprints next to it as if dozens of strong men had pulled it toward the deep pit in the middle of the night.

Running faster through the mist with Kaboo ahead of her, Aisha held back tears, her heartbeat increasing rapidly. She tried to understand why the Rock had been taken. As they neared the chasm, she feared that the Rock must have been pushed into it, now lost forever.

While they were running, the mist cleared completely, and not far ahead was the chasm. They ran past one of the hundreds of signs that stood in the ground, warning all who came near about the dangers of getting close to the death pit just beyond them. Still, they pressed closer. The first to arrive near the pit, Kaboo had gotten on his belly, scooted carefully toward to the edge and was looking into the deep darkness. The bewildered children could see the trail in the sand leading over the edge. Aisha imagined the kind Rock falling into the darkness for no reason. "No!" she cried out. "Why would they do that?"

A man's deep voice from behind them suddenly cut through the air, scaring all of them. Turning around quickly, they expected to see one of the evil men who had pushed the Rock over the edge. Standing before them was a huge man, the biggest they had ever seen. He was certainly large enough to have pushed the Rock into the death pit all by himself. The knees of the kids went weak at the sight of this unknown stranger, and Rolly and Missy crumpled onto the ground in fear, whimpering. But Kaboo instantly recognized him—the Shining man from his dream—but he didn't say a word. The man was taller than anyone they had ever seen, and his clothes glowed as if they had surging waves of electricity flowing through them.

"Please come away from the pit," the large man urged, "and don't be afraid." The shining man spoke in a clear and powerful voice that shook the insides of the frightened children.

"I will not harm you," he said with a soft voice, grinning. "I've come here to bring you a message."

The Door

Aisha somehow knew that this man was not the one who threw the Rock into the pit. He was trying to help. He was a messenger.

"I know that you are looking for the Rock who came to free Dulu," he said. "Religious men have killed him, pushing him into the darkness, but they didn't understand what they were doing," he said, pausing once again. The shining man then bent down toward the small children, leaning their way. "But I'll tell you a secret," he whispered with a confident grin. "The Rock is alive!"

"Alive?!" Aisha questioned. "Where?"

"Who are you?" Kaboo boldly interrupted, asking the man from his dream.

"I am the servant of the Ancient One," he said, glancing to his left toward the tall mountain reaching up into the sky and then back at them. "I was sent to comfort you with these words," he said, pausing again. The children waited in silence, wondering what he was talking about.

Softly he spoke again while looking toward the chasm behind them, "The Rock has now become the Door. Come and see," he said with a smile. The children stared at him, awestruck by the power and light and everything that he was saying. He began walking parallel to the pit.

The mercy winds picked up and blew upon them, flowing across the pit from Magnifikiyah against the side of their faces, blowing their hair.

The shining man pointed to something near the pit a short distance away. Ahead, the children saw a spectacular bridge that stretched all the way across the chasm to the distant side, a bridge that never existed in all of the ages from the beginning. On the front of the bridge was a small door suspended in the air. The shining man smiled at them and nodded as if answering a question they did not ask. "The One who rose from the pit has made a way for you to cross over to the other side. You can go to the Ancient One now!"

Just as the shining man spoke, he vanished with only a small, glimmering bubble in the place he had been. The bubble softly floated in the mercy winds up into the air and the morning sun. Gasping, the children looked at one another to make sure they were all really seeing and hearing this, both terrified and excited at the same time. They looked around in every direction for the shining man and could not see him.

"THE ONE WHO ROSE FROM THE PIT HAS MADE A WAY FOR YOU TO CROSS OVER TO THE
OTHER SIDE. YOU CAN GO TO THE ANCIENT ONE NOW!"

Lucas stepped forward, at first walking toward the bridge and then running while the others followed. As they got closer, the closed Door in front of the bridge came into clearer view. The Door was not tall, made only for those the size of children, but it was beautiful, radiantly blue in color and seemingly wet and alive in the morning sun. The frame of the Door had three ancient markings upon it, one on each side and one at the top, which were all glowing red.

Walking even closer and staring at this incredible Door directly in front of the bridge, Lucas and Missy suddenly fell to the ground on their knees, followed by Kaboo. The insides of the children felt like they were going to burst with emotion, and for some strange reason, they couldn't help but bow to the ground in front of this Door. They felt the overwhelming presence of love in the air, love that you could touch and feel. The same strong love that came from the Rock was now flowing from the Door, drawing the three to Himself. Somehow, just like at the Rock, the Door began communicating to the hearts of Lucas, Missy and Kaboo. Some began to say they were sorry for lying to their parents or stealing candy or being mean to others. But their sadness vanished quickly, and they too felt alive on the inside like never before. Kaboo even started to laugh out loud. His laughter touched the funny bone in everyone, and all of the children started to laugh, mostly at the sound of Kaboo's laugh.

As Kaboo laughed, the mercy winds began blowing stronger once again, and the children could hear the songs in the winds louder than ever before. It was like balls of cotton had been removed from their ears. The voices from the winds sounded something like singing waterfalls. The winds blew stronger, and the children all found themselves beginning to sing with the winds. Most of the kids were not singers, especially not the boys. But they couldn't help it. They had to sing with the winds that were singing loudly all around them, swirling around their bodies like invisible dancers.

The song came from deep within all of them, bubbling out of them like water squeezed from a bottle. Softly at first they began to sing, and then louder and louder, not caring what anyone else thought. Oddly, their voices flowed with the same melody and the same words. Lucas looked over at Aisha and saw that her words became like sparkling ribbons of light coming out of her mouth, softly floating in the air. The light ribbons, like long lightning bugs, moved through the air until they reached the Door and were absorbed by it. Lucas's face spread wide with a huge smile as he sang. Their song then rose even louder, as if an invisible choir had suddenly joined them all around, worshipping the beautiful Door that was attracting all of the sounds and light. As they sang, the Door began to breathe in and out with life, swelling larger and then smaller, larger and smaller. An amber mist began glowing all around Him in the air. Words like small rivers continued to rush out of them as they sang with all of their hearts like they had never sung before.

Suddenly, the skies burst open as if a doorway to an invisible room where the stars lived had opened up, and the most incredible thing they had ever seen filled the air. Thousands and thousands of other children, adults and shining men joined them above, singing with them the same song. They could see other people in the air! As far as they could see, the sky was a massive auditorium full of faces, and raised hands waved in the air. It was as if millions of people had come to the same concert for the small Door.

The Door

The kids looked at one another in shock with huge eyes. This didn't seem real, yet they couldn't stop singing. Their hearts flooded their mouths with amazing song and sounds—even Kaboo joined them.

The Door radiated with light, and its blue wood glistened. Closing her eyes, Aisha could hear among the thousands of people the sounds of birds and flappings of creatures all around her. Rolly glanced down for a moment and noticed that the sand was glowing, releasing small bubbles of sound toward the Door. The kids looked around them, and they felt transported to another planet.

Beyond the bridge, Magnifikiyah trembled with a quake through all of the land, and the clouds around His heights grew brighter. For what seemed like more than an hour, the song flowed, fluctuating in volume and resonating with sounds never before heard in Dulu, as the children all sang in wonder and praise. It was as if the evil of the death pit didn't exist, even though it was only a few feet away and Dulu was somewhere else. The Door was the focus of the concert.

After a long time, the sounds of singing began fading. The Sun was now a little higher in the sky.

As the songs of the thousands disappeared and the door to the sky closed, the children found themselves sitting on the ground in front of the Door. Then it was quiet. They sat in silence, quiet for awhile. No words were needed or could be said, just smiles, happy tears and wonder basking.

With the same voice as the Rock, the Door began speaking softly to each of them. He invited them to walk through Him and over the bridge. The beautiful Door slowly began to move, swinging open all by itself. Then a burst of breath came from the Door, shooting out like a blast of winter snow. The breath turned into millions of small words that fell gently upon the bridge, covering it from one end to the other, showing the way.

Aisha stood to her feet, unafraid, and walked up to the Door. She looked at the bridge ahead and then once more at the Door. The Door said, "You must believe, Aisha." The rest of the children looked on in amazement.

"Walk upon my Words and you will reach the other side safely," the Door confidently spoke inside of her. At this, Aisha's heart grew strong, and she fixed her eyes on the words lying on the path. She bent slightly, stepped through the Door and took her first step over the abyss.

One by one, they approached the Door and received words from Him that comforted them and gave them enough courage to cross over the great pit where no one had ever gone before.

Halfway over the bridge, Aisha glanced over the side of the bridge into the dark abyss. For a moment, terror gripped her heart. Her hands began to sweat, and her legs became weak. She thought of the horrors she had heard about what was in the pit and being devoured if she fell in. Then she felt a surge of soothing heat shoot up from the words through her shoes and into her feet, flowing up her ankles. She glanced up toward Nifi and felt His love drawing her across the bridge, and she continued walking. One at a time, the rest of the children walked through the Door, forming a string of six moving across the gleaming bridge that connected the land of Dulu with the land of Nifi.

Chapter Three

LAND OF NIFI

All of the children made it over the bottomless chasm, cheering one another on as the last ones stepped onto the soil of the Magnifikiyah and into the land of Nifi for the very first time. They celebrated with high fives and hugs like they had just won the duluball championship. They were walking in a place that no one they knew of had ever been.

Their first breaths of air in this land cleared their minds instantly. The air was crisp and clean, and the land was lush, with tall green trees, waving grass and vibrant flowers. It seemed as if they had traveled into a different world and nothing was impossible.

Ahead of them was Nifi, the rugged mountain towering brightly above them, larger and more real than ever but still covered with flashing bursts of light among the high-elevation mist. Nifi seemed more powerful and so much larger here—even more fearful. Aisha turned around to glance back toward Dulu, hardly believing where she now was. She looked at the bridge they had just crossed and the abyss below it, grinning from ear to ear.

Were they really on the other side of the pit? How could this really be? It was the best dream coming true. She thought about her parents and how difficult it was to convince them that the Rock was alive. There was no way that they would believe this story.

Dulu looked so hazy and barren compared to the land of Nifi. Aisha turned back toward the mountain again and everything was clear, free of any haze.

They were really at the feet of Nifi, and the eyes of the children glimmered with expectation of what might be ahead. Energy and excitement were almost too much to contain. They felt a sense of unlocked adventure and impossibility. Amazed that they were actually in the land of Nifi, Kaboo said,

"What are we waiting for? Come on!" He took off running, followed by the rest of the kids, tearing through the meadows of tall green grass.

The children ran around, shouting loudly as they touched grass and feeling free for the very first time in their lives. They rolled around in the meadow and stared at vibrant flowers, breathing in their fragrance that seemed to tingle inside of their bodies. Flowers of every color and size were mixed in with the tall, waving grass. The faces of the flowers seemed to turn and follow them as they passed, appearing to smile back at them as the girls bent over to smell them. The girls began making beautiful bouquets, while the boys ran through the grass like wild horses, galloping and chasing one another.

The children could hear rushing water ahead, and Kaboo led the way to the top of a small hill. Stretching before them was a peaceful river winding through the meadow, smooth and calm.

"Look at that!" shouted Lucas, as fish larger than people swam and jumped out of the crystal river in front of them. Stories from the ancient books about the fish that people used to ride in the old days flooded Lucas' mind. He could now imagine himself doing the same.

All of the children ran down to the river to get a closer look at the strange creatures. As they cautiously neared the water, one of the fish suddenly surfaced and plopped his large head on the shore, splashing the kids, soaking them and causing them to jump backwards in frightful surprise. Missy grabbed onto Lucas tightly and stared at the creature while hiding behind him, unsure if they were about to be attacked by a river creature.

The fish was a beautiful bright blue and yellow, with pink and white markings. Its head was rounded and its skin was smooth like a dolphin. It looked at them like a puppy would, seemingly happy to see them.

Kaboo took a step forward and the fish didn't move, his eyes fixed on Kaboo. He carefully took another step even closer. Suddenly, the fish opened its mouth and, with a squeaky human voice, playfully spoke: "C'mon, I'll give you a ride."

Kaboo smiled back at the rest of the kids for a moment with a look of disbelief. Isabelle and the others giggled and gasped in unbelief. Kaboo walked over and threw his leg over the back of the

SUDDENLY, THE FISH OPENED ITS MOUTH AND WITH A SQUEAKY HUMAN VOICE, PLAYFULLY SPOKE: "C'MON, I'LL GIVE YOU A RIDE."

fish. The fish was wet and slick to the touch but just the perfect size to ride. The fish said, "Hold on tightly," and Kaboo grabbed his fins with his hands, squeezing his legs against the side of the creature. The fish wiggled backwards, then sideways, and took off through the water with a splash and a hard kick of his tail, splashing those watching. Kaboo held on for dear life, yelling like he was riding a wild pubba.

They went entirely under water for a moment, and then they came up and stayed on the surface, darting around the river. Other fish were summoned to the fun, surfacing and jumping over Kaboo like they were at a playground.

Several other fish came near the shoreline and landed on the bank, inviting the other kids to take a ride. Rolly, Lucas and Isabelle ran forward and jumped on fish, while Missy stayed on the shore with Aisha, unsure and unconfident in the water.

The fish said nothing but gently took the children out into the water, joining Kaboo and swimming all around to the children's delight.

After swimming around to their hearts' content, the children were brought back to the shore. Kaboo began talking with his fish and asked him what his name was. The fish said, "My name is Drenjee, and I'm a Holissafren. We Holissafrens were made to have fun. Come swim with us anytime, young rider. You ride well, and we can do some higher leaps next time you come."

"That would be awesome!" exclaimed Kaboo with a laugh. "Thank you for taking me for a swim," he said, hardly believing that he was actually talking to a fish. "I am Kaboo, and I want to do this everyday!" The other Holissafrens brought their wet and happy riders back to the shore, all of them breathing hard, soaking wet and grinning wildly.

As soon as the children got off the fish, the Holissafrens flopped back into the river and jumped into the air for a parting splash before slipping back under the water. The kids cheered and laughed at these incredible creatures. Missy ran to Lucas to make sure he was okay and hugged her big, wet brother.

"I'm fine Missy," Lucas said. "That was a blast! I can't believe we just did that. Next time you should do it, too." He shook the excess water off of him, pulled his clinging shirt away from his stomach and began to dry in the warm sun. Missy felt a bit sad

Dulu

that she didn't join in but was relieved that they were moving on.

As they were about to go, the sky suddenly darkened and then lit back up again as the shadow of something large passed overhead. The children heard a screech and instinctively drew close together while the largest bird they had ever seen flew overhead toward the great Mountain.

"What was that?" whispered Rolly, obviously alarmed at such a large bird flying so near to them.

"I don't know," said Lucas, "but I don't think it's dangerous, or it would have eaten us just now. It's probably just as happy as the Holissafrens. Let's keep going."

Looking toward the mountain in the distance was a tall, streaming waterfall. The kids ran toward their next new discovery and found the waterfall to be much taller than the largest building they had ever seen in Dulu. The water fell hundreds of feet before crashing onto rocks and then dropping again even further toward the bottom. The falls became louder with every step. As they neared the rushing waters, a misty spray fell upon their faces, blowing little drops of clear water onto their hair. Isabelle exclaimed, "This is beautiful!" She stretched her hands into the air to feel the mist and smiled from ear to ear.

Next to the falls was the beginning of a great forest with huge trees growing like pillars into the sky along the meadow. "Wow!" exclaimed Rolly, walking away from the falls toward enormous trunks emerging from the ground. He reached out to touch the thick bark that coated the skyward giants, bending his neck upwards trying to see the top and nearly falling over backwards. The dardruk trees back in Dulu were barely as high as their homes. It would take ten Dulu trees on top of each other to be as tall as the monster conifers here. Each tree was more than a dozen feet wide, with ridges of flowing bark rising up to the limbs high above.

Everywhere the children looked, there seemed to be something magnificent, new and unexpected—things that neither their eyes nor their imaginations had beheld. This place was a feast for their senses, and the children were indulging. In the midst of the beauty all around them, each one felt a strange desire to climb all the way to the top of the mountain itself to get near the face of the Ancient One where the Rock had been before He rolled down to them.

While walking among the giants along the edge of the meadow, Kaboo suddenly pointed ahead of them. Standing in the distance was a man with a stick in His hand. This was the first human they had seen in the land of Nifi, and they were curious to speak with Him, to find out if He had followed them across the bridge. Nearing the man, Missy whispered quietly, "Do you think He is friendly? Why does He have a stick in his hand?"

All eyes were fixed upon Him as they carefully approached. Missy peered around Lucas while staying close behind him. Once nearer, the kids could see that He was dressed strangely compared to the rest of them, clothed with a tan robe and a leather belt. Clearly, He wasn't from Dulu. He had been watching them the whole time they were in the meadow, quietly enjoying their running through the grass and riding the Holissafrens. As the children walked closer, their fears diminished as they felt such a peace and safety exuding from Him like they did at the Rock and the Door.

"Hello," the stranger in the strange clothes said with a smile as they came closer, His words piercing their heart with hope and peace, His eyes gleaming brightly—clear and intense. This man had dark hair and light brown skin, much like Aisha had, with beautiful and penetrating brown eyes. He gave the children a smile and sat down in the grass that overlooked the river and meadow, inviting them to do the same. They approached carefully and then sat down. At first no one said a word; they just stared at Him. All of the children felt like they knew this man, but they had never seen Him before.

While the others were staring at Him, being fed by the warmth in His eyes and smile, Missy crawled closer to Him than the rest. She said, "Who are you?" and leaned forward with a grin. The man touched her gently on the head with His strong hand and said, "I am the Good Shepherd. I shepherd all the flocks owned by my Father, the Ancient One."

"And you are Melissa, but everyone calls you Missy," He said to her with a half-smile.

Missy's mouth dropped open in amazement.

"How do you know my name?" Missy asked, feeling special more than scared because He knew her name.

"Oh, I have known all about you from before you were ever born," He said confidently. "But at the Rock and at the Door, you began to know me." The children were quickly taken back in their minds to the time that they first heard His voice speak to them, and at that moment they all knew that this Good Shepherd was also the same Rock and the Door who had led them here somehow. But now He was human.

Missy then dove into His arms, followed by Rolly and the rest of them, and they began gasp and laugh like they had just met their big brother who had been away on a long journey and had finally returned. Their laughter echoed through the meadow, and the grass seemed to wave with them in joy. The children each began to talk to the Good Shepherd excitedly, and they asked Him all kinds of questions. They asked how the Rock came to Dulu and if He got dizzy rolling down the mountain. They asked about the bridge and Aisha's mom's knee. For what seemed like an hour, the Good Shepherd shared with them the answers to most of their questions and how He and his Father had been watching Dulu since it began.

The children stared at Him intensely as He shared why He had been sent to Dulu. The sheep behind them that had been eating grass came close, standing around listening to the story they loved to hear. Rolly glanced at the face of one of the sheep, and the sheep winked at him, appearing to smile as well. Rolly glanced at the other kids, hoping they saw this too, but they didn't.

The Shepherd shared of his Father's great love for the people of Dulu, a love so strong that it broke Him away from the side of the Ancient One. It sent Him rolling down the mountain and into the sands of Dulu—through time and distance, to seek and save the lost. He spoke of His Father's longing for the people of Dulu to come across the pit of death and visit with Him, high up on the mountain.

The Good Shepherd also spoke of an evil enemy who flew around in the air of Dulu as a thief of hope, the destroyer of dreams and the twister of truth. He called this thief "the Liar." The Liar now lived invisibly in the air above Dulu, turning the air a hazy rust color, making the things they see seem different than what they really were—especially Nifi. The Shepherd said that though the Liar was full of hate and fear, the children should never be afraid of the Liar.

"But why shouldn't we be afraid of the Liar?" asked Missy.

Stretching His hand out and touching her head lightly, He said, "Because I have already defeated him. I am much stronger than he is. Even more importantly, you shouldn't fear because my Father and I love and watch over you, just as we have been doing your entire life. Our love for you is greater than all of the hatred he has for you."

The Good Shepherd explained that the Liar was the one who caused all sickness in Dulu and who was always whispering lies into the ears of the people. He was also the one who stirred the men to push the Rock into the pit. As the Shepherd spoke of the pit, Aisha turned to see if she could see it from where they were. All she could see was a hazy dark cloud that hovered in the distance over Dulu. *This must be the cloud of lies that comes from the Liar and hangs over Dulu*, she thought to herself. She also noticed that the air didn't look hazy when they were in Dulu, but now the haze was visible.

After a long time of talking, laughing and having fun with the Good Shepherd, Isabelle asked

Him if He could take them to see the Ancient One. He smiled and confidently said, "Yes, I will lead you to Him. The invitation is always open, but you must choose to go yourself. Come, follow me. I am the Way." He stood to his feet. The children quickly did the same.

He turned and began walking into the trees. As soon as He came under the canopy of the forest, He tripped and fell forward onto His face. Lucas lurched forward along with the others to see if He was okay and to help Him get back up. All of the children felt a concern for Him as they surrounded Him. Then, before their eyes, He suddenly transformed into the Way before them, stretching up through the forest as a lighted pathway for them to walk upon.

"He has changed form again," said Lucas. "He's now the Pathway." Amazed at all they had just learned and how the Shepherd had just shifted into another shape, they looked at one another and carefully stepped onto the Way, hoping it wouldn't hurt Him. As far as they could see through the trees, the Way led up the mountain. Walking on the Way reminded them of the bridge that was covered with His words they had crossed over the pit.

At first, the Way was very clear and bright, but as it wound up through the forest, it seemed to grow more faint as they traveled, requiring them to focus.

Light was everywhere in this beautiful land. The soil, the trees and even the stones on the ground emanated with a soft light and wonderful smell. They walked effortlessly over a hill and up one steeper still on the other side. Many streams of water crossed the Way they were walking upon, and the children enjoyed every step, stopping often to drink from the clear waters or admire every form of creation along the path.

A strange wail followed by a cracking noise suddenly sounded above them in the air among the tall trees. The children froze, staring up into the sky, waiting to see what creature had made the strange noise. Again they heard the sound, but now the noise was coming from all around them. Looking around quickly to see what was generating the spooky noise, the children pressed closer to one another, sensing the presence of something living coming nearer.

Lucas said firmly, "Stay together and don't move." The eerie sound coming from a flying animal of some kind echoed directly overhead. The animal flew at an amazing speed above them, springing from the large trees with long legs and then soaring around before bouncing off of another tree, nearly making them dizzy as they tried to follow him. Many more creatures appeared among the trees, bouncing and flying around in a blur, filling the air with their loud call. Suddenly, one of the creatures dropped to the earth like a stone and landed in front of them with a *thud*! The children jumped back and stared at the creature, which looked like a cross between a lemur and a bird and stood about four feet high. He curiously tilted his head, stared back at them and raised his furry arms into the air, his large, sparkling green eyes fixed on them.

Suddenly, several dozen other creatures dropped to the ground all around them. *Thud, thud, thud*! They landed to the ground, surrounding the children, and folded their wings.

In a cheerful, raspy and high-pitched voice, the first creature said, "Welcome creatures of Dulu! Sambiniis we are—some of the many creatures of the trees." He stepped even closer, nearly touching Aisha, and looked at her with great curiosity. "We have been waiting a long time for you to come to Nifi," he said and then paused, staring at her. "You are strange-looking little warriors," he chuckled, "with soft skin." Leaning closer to Aisha, the lead Sambinii began sniffing her bare arm, his soft, wet nose tickling her arm like her puppy. "Smells like one of His children!"

The other Sambiniis came closer to the children to smell them also. They looked curiously up and down them like they were staring at Martians. One of the Sambiniis even put his furry little hand on Rolly's hand and felt his hairless fingers.

Seemingly satisfied, the lead Sambinii took a step backward and looked at all of the children. "May you enjoy Magnifikiyah and the power of His kingdom!" the Sambinii announced. The other Sambiniis erupted in loud bursts that echoed through the trees. He bowed slightly toward the children, acknowledging and honoring the children of the Ancient One. All of the other Saminiis did the same.

The children smiled and looked at one another, thoroughly enjoying these friendly creatures. Aisha really wanted to take one home with her. They were the cutest and friendliest creatures she had ever seen.

"Thank you," Lucas said to them on behalf of all six of the children.

"*Ooweee!*" The leading Sambinii let out a loud sound that echoed through the forest. He jumped far into the air and bounced off of the nearest tree, soaring around them before flying away. The other Sambiniis followed and also jumped into the air, flying around the children and then up high into the forest, their noise echoing through the trees as they left.

"Wow!" said Rolly. "Those were cool. I was a little afraid when they first started hitting the ground, but they were really friendly."

"They are so cute," said Aisha. "I was hoping that they would stay longer so we could speak with them more or that they would come with us."

"I have a feeling we'll see them again," said Kaboo. "Let's see what is ahead," he said, looking up the path, which was now hardly visible. The path, which had been very bright in the beginning, was now dimmer but just as real as ever. The children began to sense the path was there more than they could see it.

They moved forward again along the Way, which turned a corner up ahead, leading underneath a large rock cliff. The trees swayed back and forth like they, too, were following the children with invisible eyes, yet there was no fear in this place; they were happy trees.

Kaboo and Lucas had run ahead a little ways and suddenly began yelling for the others. "Come here and look at this, you guys!" Kaboo exclaimed excitedly. Just on the right side of the Way was a large bubbling spring surrounded by smooth stones, with several other pools like it all around. A moist, soothing vapor rose into the air from each pool, turning amber in color as it flowed up toward the sky. Next to the pools, the Way looked different and almost torn. There were several red markings that seemed like claw marks across it, and looking at the marks made them feel a sense of great pain or torture. It looked as if a giant lion had scratched the path, and from the marks flowed dark red waters that dripped into the bubbling springs like large vats of wine.

All of the children began to take their shoes off and roll their pants up. They sat along the glowing pool's edge, slowly placing their feet into its steamy waters. While Aisha took her sandals off, she heard the Good Shepherd speak inside of her: "These are the healing pools that came from my wounds." She looked around for a moment and didn't see Him, but her eyes were drawn to the claw marks in the path, which were glimmering in the sunbeams that had penetrated the forest canopy.

"Healing Pools—these are called the Healing Pools," she said out loud, growing in confidence that the Good Shepherd had just spoken to her. The children moved their legs around in the soothing waters, inhaling the menthol-like vapors from the pool into their souls. The ache of their feet went away, and not a muscle or joint in them felt tired or sore.

Kaboo had broken his nose jumping off a play set when he was only two years old, but he suddenly felt the knots on his nose shrink, and his nose straightened into place without pain. He drew a deep breath through His nose, and the air moved freely into his lungs. "My nose!" he cried, holding it with both hands. "I can breathe again, and the bumps are gone."

The palms of Isabelle's hands began to get very warm, like she had placed them into invisible electric gloves. She looked at them, and they were red with oil glistening upon them. Lucas looked at Isabelle and quickly saw a moving picture in his mind that startled him a bit but was so very real.

"Isabelle," Lucas said a bit shyly.

"Yes," she replied quietly, distracted by and still staring at the oil running out of her hands.

"This may sound strange, but as I looked at you, I saw something in my mind like a dream, but I was awake," Lucas said. "It was like seeing a movie in my mind. I could see you touching people, and they were getting healed by some sort of power. You touched an older man with white eyes, and color came into his eyes. A young boy also came to you with a damaged arm that was cut off or something, and when you touched him, his arm began to grow out, long and straight. Then fingers popped out of his hand!" The children around the pool listened intently; chills ran up their spines and amazement filled their hearts.

LAND OF NIFI

Aisha suddenly felt a need to forgive the Brock twins for how mean they had been to her. As she thought of them in her mind, compassion grew in her heart, and she felt like the Good Shepherd wanted her to forgive them. Inwardly, she said, *I forgive both of you.* That moment, Aisha felt the warm water from the pool rise up her legs, through her body and into her heart, cleansing it all over again. She sighed heavily and felt like a new person.

While the children pondered all of these things, Kaboo began splashing everyone with water from the pool.

"Hey, knock it off," Isabelle said to Kaboo. The others joined in, telling him to stop.

"I was just having some fun," Kaboo said.

About that time, Missy noticed that butterflies were filling the air. Butterflies of every color and size fluttered through the trees, invading the air all around them as a silent army. Some were as wide as the door they had walked through earlier, and others were much smaller. Looking up toward the trees, these silent creatures swarmed the heavens by the thousands, many landing on the children's heads, shoulders and noses. Missy began giggling while one bright blue and green butterfly with large yellow and purple spots sat on her shoulder and began whispering into her ear. She could not understand the odd noises coming from the butterfly, and it seemed surprised that she didn't speak the butterfly language, so it fluttered away.

Many of the butterflies landed all around the pools and paused to drink from the drops of water formed on the edge. Thousands of others landed on the ground and the trees all around them. The forest seemed to be covered like a blanket by these peaceful creatures, and the ground appeared to be breathing as the ever-moving wings moved slowly up and down. The girls all began giggling, but Kaboo wasn't impressed. He liked larger animals and had never been much for butterflies or flowers or things like that—even if these butterflies were as large as birds and incredibly colorful.

After several minutes of giggling and listening to the butterflies' strange whisperings, the rabble of colorful animals filled the air again and ascended toward the top of the trees, once again on the move.

A short while later, the children again felt the drawing of the Ancient One, and they began to dry their feet and put on their shoes. Stepping back onto the Way, they felt refreshed and healthy, inside and out. They had no grudges against anyone, and their minds were constantly filled with good thoughts, not thoughts of doubt, fear, worry or comparison.

The path was nearly invisible now, but the children could all sense that it was still there, leading them higher and higher. They walked until they emerged from the dense forest and came to a lofty ridge. The children found themselves among large outcrops of granite rock with a cliff on their right. Gusts of wind blew from different directions as they neared the edge. From this place the view was incredible. The children could see all of the land of Dulu and the chasm far below that looked like a small black snake winding through the sand. The homes in Dulu were specks in the distance, and the land looked dry and dark—lifeless compared to where they were now.

Kaboo spotted a massive Eagle with enormous wings suddenly approaching just in front of them, rising quickly on the strong updrafts that lifted him up beside the mountain cliffs. The children once again moved toward one another for safety.

The giant eagle was headed right for them and seemed to be looking at them. He looked large enough to carry any one of them away! Just before reaching the children, he turned his heavy wings and flew northward while looking intently at them. His intense eyes were piercing and nearly glowing, seeming to peer into their souls. He made a wide circle in the air and then came toward them again, this time landing his enormous body only a few feet away from them. The shale rock shifted under his weight. The presence of such a large creature so close to them was intimidating.

The height of the eagle was nearly ten feet, and Lucas imagined that the long talons and powerful beak could tear apart a full-grown pubba in only seconds. The children clung to one another, motionless. They stared at the bird while he stared back at them, and the winds blew his pure white neck feathers. The eagle took another step closer, still peering intensely with penetrating eyes, and then he tilted his head and sharp beak slightly.

"You shouldn't be afraid," he said to them with a voice rich and strong. "I won't harm you."

"Who...who are you? What are you?" asked Isabelle, looking up toward the fantastic creature.

"I am one who sees. I saw you at the Rock; I've been watching you as you have climbed the mountain, and I see you helping Dulu in the days ahead," he said with authority, like the mayor of Dulu was talking.

"Helping Dulu?" Kaboo questioned. "How could we help Dulu? The Liar has turned the air dark, and we are just kids."

The great bird stared intently at Kaboo without answering. Kaboo shrunk under his direct gaze and slipped behind Lucas. The eagle then spoke to Kaboo and to the rest of the children in a clear and direct voice: "Truth and love pierce the Liar's haze. Yes, you are young, but you have been chosen. Do not fear! Nothing can stop the loved."

The children glanced down at Dulu. The thick, dark haze that spread over all of the land still seemed impossible to overcome, but the words of the Eagle made something inside of them grow stronger. Something of a hope and courage.

The great eagle stepped even closer to them, his black feathers nearly touching them, and his powerful talons scratched on the rocks just inches from their own small shoes. Isabelle and Kaboo were thinking of a way to run away if the eagle decided to make a snack out of them.

Without saying a word, the creature spread his tremendous wings into the air over their heads, blocking the sun and the view of the sky. Feathers were all they could see, and it felt like they were about to be eaten. Plumage hung over them, and the smell of this magnificent creature filled the air. It was a smell unlike anything they had ever smelled—strong yet almost sweet. As their eyes adjusted to lack of light, they held one another. Fluffy little feathers began falling from the large wings above them, floating in the air and softly falling toward the ground around them. The children were hidden from all else around, almost like being inside a cozy cave. Yet there was a soft light all around them.

"Here is where you must stay," the eagle said. His voice was strong yet filled with comfort, like slipping into a large easy chair that surrounds all of you.

"Stay under my wings and see with my eyes. Here you are safe, and here your eyes will be changed to view people as I do."

WITHOUT SAYING A WORD, THE CREATURE SPREAD HIS TREMENDOUS WINGS INTO THE AIR OVER THEIR HEADS, BLOCKING THE SUN AND THE VIEW OF THE SKY.

It seemed strange that he was talking about seeing when they couldn't see anything but feathers at the moment, but the children felt safe and very secure. If war were raging around them, even that could not disturb the peace that filled the air and their hearts in this impenetrable fortress of feathers. It was as peaceful and as restful as sleeping, yet they were awake, soothed by the presence of the strong bird.

After many minutes, the eagle began to lift his wings. The bright sun shone on their faces again, and the children squinted and blocked the sun with their hands while they waited for their eyes to readjust. Suddenly, they heard a deep whooshing sound as the raptor turned and jumped into the air over the edge of the cliff, his huge wings outstretched. A surging updraft gust from down below the cliff caught the bird and quickly lifted him high into the sky above. In only seconds, he was gone.

Although they were standing alone among the cliffs, the children didn't feel alone. The experience with the great eagle had changed their sight. As they looked once again down at Dulu, the thick haze remained over the entire land. Only now, the children could see through the haze as if they had extraordinary vision. The haze seemed more like a dark cloth covering a hidden prize, but now they could see treasure in Dulu. With their new sight, they looked in every direction to the far reaches of the horizon. Beyond Dulu they could somehow see countries and lands they had never heard of. They could see dozens of cities on islands and across oceans far away. Still the dark haze was over these lands, too, but the children were now able to look through darkness.

From this place high up on the mountain, the children heard low rumbles from the top of Nifi echoing down the mountain. The sounds sent shivers down their spines, but the mountain still invited them higher. They sensed some danger, but not an evil danger—only the danger of the unknown.

Chapter Five

THE ANCIENT ONE

The rumbling that shook the ground thundered down the mountain, sending slight tremors into their feet as they stood on the path. A sense of trepidation mixed with fear instantly caused goose bumps to rise on their skin. Although every fearful experience so far ended up being wonderful, knowing that they were nearing something so powerful was still scary. Nonetheless, the inner pull of the Ancient One invited them higher.

The faint path wove around the rock cliff and then steeply up between spires of stone that jutted sharply into the air. The path then led back into a more dense forest with smaller and darker green trees mixed with ferns and flowering plants of various shapes and colors.

At these heights, the air was thinner, making it more difficult to breathe. The children had never been at this altitude, and their young lungs were not used to breathing air this clean or this thin, making their trek slower than before. Missy kept slowing them down even further because she was the smallest and youngest of the kids, often calling out for the others to slow down while gasping for air and leaning against a tree or large stone.

Through the forest in the distance high above, a faint glow was emanating. The children didn't speak much during this portion of their adventure, but they were all wondering what awaited them and what the Ancient One must be like. They could feel that they were getting close. Soon the Way led to the base of massive gates that were nearly as tall as the trees.

"Oh my gosh!" exclaimed Rolly. "Look at the size of this fence and wall," he marveled, staring at and touching the base of the towering enclosure.

"That isn't a fence," Lucas corrected him. "These are gates," he said, between large gasps of air. "I've read about gates like this in some of the Ancient books."

"I hope the creature that made these things is friendly, or we're in big, big trouble," said Kaboo, as he peeked through the gates, trying to see what was on the other side.

"He will be," Aisha said in a convincing tone while looking up at them. "These are the gates of the Ancient One," she said. "He is somewhere beyond here, and we have to find a way through."

The gate walls were glowing white in color with a light of their own. They had one massive door mounted with great hinges and unique and unknown designs carved into the pillars. The door of the gate was firmly closed, and the children looked like ants next the structure.

Standing in front of the gates, the children were not only amazed at the size, but also perplexed at how to get through. Lucas said, "I wonder if we should stop here and turn around since we can't get through. It's getting late, and we should probably start heading back before it gets dark. We've been gone a long time, and I'm sure our parents are wondering where we are and very worried."

Lucas, the oldest child and big brother of Missy, had a sense of responsibility for her and all of the children and wanted to make sure that no one got in trouble.

"Turn around? Are you crazy?" responded Kaboo. "We can't turn around here. We're almost to the top," he exclaimed. "I'm going to find a way through these gates, even if I have to climb over them," he said while looking to see if he could squeeze through one of the holes in the gate.

"Look at the sun," Rolly said while motioning into the sky. "It's still high up in the sky. It seems like we have been here for days, but I don't even think it is lunchtime yet."

Lucas looked down at his wristwatch to check the time. "10:10 am," he said out loud. "How can that be?" He questioned his watch and flicked it with his finger as if he were trying to get it to work. "We have been walking for many hours now. There must be something wrong with this thing."

"I don't think so," said Aisha. "I don't think time is important in this place. I think we are just supposed to keep going and not worry about it right now."

THE DOOR OF THE GATE WAS FIRMLY CLOSED, AND THE CHILDREN LOOKED LIKE ANTS NEXT THE STRUCTURE.

Dulu

Lucas looked at Missy, who was smiling at him, agreeing with Aisha.

"Please Lucas, let's keep going. We'll make it back in time," she said.

Lucas stared at his watch, then the sky, then the closed gates again and said, "I don't know." He pondered while glancing down toward Dulu for a moment. "Maybe we can go just a few minutes more if we can find a way through the gates," he said, unsure if it was the right decision.

The children could all sense that the path continued through the gates, but there appeared to be no way to follow it. On either side of the narrow path was a sheer drop off and no way around the gate.

The gate had no handle or lock, and they could not climb over it or go around it. Unlike the Door in Dulu that was just their size, this gate was for giants.

Suddenly, their feet began to tingle for a moment, and the Way seemed to become visible. Missy dropped to her hands and knees to look more closely at the Way, and she noticed something for the first time.

The Ancient One

"Hey you guys! There are words on this path," Missy declared, excited to find something before the others did.

Rolly bent down and gazed at the path. "I wonder if there is a secret code or password somewhere here that we can find," he said, digging around with his hands. All of the children except for Kaboo (who was trying to squeeze through the gates) got down on all fours, trying to read the letters, looking at them with tilted heads and squinting eyes, swishing the stones and dirt around.

The words were like an ancient manuscript, written in another language.

"I can't read any of this," said Isabelle, becoming a little frustrated as she stared at the strange words on the path. "It's all in some other language."

Excited at the thought of a secret language from a distant land, Kaboo jumped down from the gate and started to look. He first noticed what seemed to be a faint reflection of himself among the words, but as he looked closer, he began to see movement, like faces of other living people. He began to fix his eyes on the faces until he recognized an older woman. The image was a bit fuzzy, but the longer he stared, the more clear her face became. Then he recognized her. The woman was his grandmother!

His Grammy was kneeling in prayer next to a chair, and he began to hear the words she was saying, as if she were right next to him. She was asking the Ancient One to save and protect her grandson Kaboo! He then saw her prayers over the years rolled into a moment. He saw himself lying on the ground in front of the Door from earlier that morning. It was then that he understood. Kaboo began whispering, "Thank you, Ancient One, for listening to the prayers of my grandmother. Thank you for helping me." A rush came into his heart, and a tear dropped from his eye onto the path.

"I see something!" Missy shrieked while she stared at the path. "It's not the words—there are people inside the words!" she exclaimed with wonder.

The children began to see the faces of people as though the path had become a 3-D movie theater. Images of faces and places flashed from the path, captivating the children. They were now so real and so vivid that Isabelle reached out her hand to touch the person she was seeing. Her hand and arm seemed to go right into the ground and into the scene, yet her hand was not visible. They recognized some but not all of the people. Lucas saw his parents, while others saw a teacher from school or someone who had helped or guided them in life.

Other images showed elderly people they had never seen before being killed or harmed for loving the Ancient One. The children knew that somehow even those they didn't know were suffering for them. They saw images of the Rock rolling down the Ancient One and then being dragged away and thrown into the pit.

A story was told with each image about how much they were all loved and how so many had helped them get to the foot of the massive gates that stood in front of them. The children's hearts were melted, and they felt so thankful for all that had been done for them, even before they were born. Simultaneously, the children looked up toward the mountain and began crying out in thankfulness to the invisible Ancient One, hoping He could hear them beyond those gates.

Choruses of thanksgiving echoed through the cracks in the gates, traveling up the mountain.

"Thank you for sending the Rock and for the life that He gave for me," Isabelle cried out. "Thank you for my parents and grandparents who prayed for me. Thank you for your love, for taking away all of my hurts. Thank you for hearing every prayer."

Suddenly a loud noise like the thundering of steel breaking apart burst from within the midst of the gates and echoed through the woods. The children jumped backward at the explosive sound. Slowly, the massive structure began to move away from them on its own, as if by some magic power.

"Oh my gosh!" Rolly and Isabelle exclaimed together. "They are opening!" The children watched as the huge gates swung open with a deep-sounding creak.

Kaboo jumped through the open entrance and onto the other side with an excited shout and then smiled at the rest of the children in celebration.

While walking through the door, Aisha said, "Thanks," under her breath. "That's why the gates opened!" she exclaimed loudly. "The key that opens the gates of the Ancient One is *thanks*."

"How do you know that?" asked Isabelle.

"Because I just heard the Rock—I mean, the Good Shepherd—tell me," Aisha replied.

"Really?" asked Lucas, staring up at the wide open door, amazed at how words of thanks could move such powerful doors.

For the first time, the children realized that they were in this place not by chance or because of their bravery, but because of the love of the Ancient One and what He had done for them.

The Way now led even higher, disappearing into the thick clouds they had all seen from Dulu. They knew they were close. The air became still and calm as they took their first steps into the fluffy mist. They each held hands as they entered the thick misty clouds, and a joy trickled down through them all over again.

Anticipation caused them to pick up the pace, yet the clouds were flashing just ahead of them, urging caution. Isabelle felt the sudden desire to begin singing again. As she did, the other kids joined in. At first the singing was soft and calming, but quickly it changed to a song with shouts like a blast from a trumpet. The new song came from within them and was mixed with shouts of praise and bragging of the kindness of the Ancient One.

All of a sudden, real trumpets and blasts of noise and voices they had never heard before roared up ahead, responding to their song. The children continued to shout, and then, somewhere in the clouds ahead of them, others shouted back at them. It felt as though they were about to join a gigantic party with thousands of people they didn't know.

Then suddenly, all fell silent and still. They stopped singing, and sounds of celebration in the distance ceased as well. The clouds darkened slightly and then slowly drew away from around them. Standing only feet away from them was the most magnificent creature they had ever seen. The children gasped, frozen in place. The girls covered their mouths with their hands. The creature in front of them could only be described as a lion, yet he was different from a lion. His large head and flowing mane were impressive, and the muscles in his body were defined and bulging with power. Although he looked like a lion, this creature had numerous eyes around his head and even inside his body, peering through his own skin. The eyes were looking in many directions at the same time. The tail on the creature was twitching slightly as he sat on his hindquarters just in front of them, and

STANDING ONLY FEET AWAY FROM THEM WAS THE MOST
MAGNIFICENT CREATURE THEY HAD EVER SEEN.

he stared at them with several of his eyes. Though seated, the creature was still nearly three or four feet taller than Lucas with feathered wings lying against his back, blending into his beautiful fur coat. The children were not afraid but still knew that if this were a hungry lion, they would become a meal.

The sound of heavy wings suddenly thrashed loudly through the air above them, as three more massive creatures descended to the ground, landing near the Lion. The floor shook under the weight as they landed. One of them looked similar to the giant eagle they had seen earlier, but this bird had numerous eyes like the lion, was darker in color and had six wings instead of two, with eyes underneath his wings. The third creature was in the shape of an ox. He was the largest of the creatures and had six wings with eyes underneath his wings. The fourth creature looked something like a large pubba, yet it had the face of a man. It had six wings with eyes scattered around underneath.

A rumble then came from deep within the lion-like creature as he tilted his head toward the destination ahead. He opened his mouth and roared out a word unlike anything the children had ever heard. The rumble echoed through the distance, sending chills up the spines of the children. They grabbed one another tightly, leaving marks on their skin. Missy's hands covered her ears, and she closed her eyes.

The other three creatures turned in the same direction and began uttering the same word through the air with their own distinct sounds, shaking the floor. As the sounds rumbled, the covering of clouds cleared in front of them, and they found themselves in a massive hall filled with bright light.

Fear and awe swept into the children, and they all fell to the floor of the court, huddling together like lumps of dough, frozen in place. In the silence, the light grew brighter and brighter, like the sun itself was flying toward them with incredible intensity. It felt for a moment that they were going to be burned up by the thick heat and power.

Then their fear of death gave way to a deep sense of love. They began to feel the unusual feeling that they were home and that they had arrived at the place they were always intended to be. The light diminished slightly, and the children looked up from the warm, soft floor. In front of them, atop many large stairs, seated upon a majestic throne and leaning slightly toward them with a smile on His face, was the Ancient One. His smile made the shining men around Him also smile with delight. There was no doubt that He was the power of the universe and the Ancient One they had been seeking. His smile made their hearts swell, growing their capacity to be loved. They were unable to speak, and they all knew that this was their Father, their real Father.

Around their Father were millions of people, some filling seats and others standing, stretching as far as they could see. There were also flying creatures that whirled around in the air, some very large with wings even bigger than the eagle's and some smaller with several wings. There were also flashes of light shooting around in the air, leaving glowing trails of sparkly light through the room.

The Ancient One stared at the children lovingly, communicating to their minds and hearts without saying a word. Abba, not Ancient One, was the name He wanted them to call Him. Everything that they had imagined about Abba was true, but it didn't begin to tell the story. Then, as if an invitation was brought to them, the children began to run toward Him at full speed with Missy in the lead. They sprang forward like kids running to greet their dad who had returned from a long journey.

They bounded up the stairs toward Him. Isabelle had the strange sensation that she had been there before. Then she remembered her experience at the Rock and wondered if that were a memory, a dream or this very moment that she had seen in the future. All six kids boldly came to Him and jumped in His large lap, each having his or her own special place on His knees.

At once, a thundering sound of great singing erupted all around them, both above and below, ringing out for miles into the distance. Light emanating from the Ancient One illuminated this great hall, revealing multiple millions of people and hundreds of thousands of creatures. Many with instruments and everyone with a voice started singing and celebrating together, worshiping the Ancient One. The floor began shaking with songs and dancing.

Streams of smaller creatures shot through the air, like bubbles of light zipping through the space, moving with the singing. The four creatures took flight also, lifting off of the ground and soaring around Abba while bellowing their rumbling words that became a part of the song.

To each of the children, this seemed like a dream in a world far away that couldn't be real. Yet looking at one another and then in Abba's eyes, they knew that this reality and the lives they had lived in Dulu must have been the dream instead.

Peals of thunder echoed in this huge chamber, and flashes of lightning bent around the seat of Abba in a circle. Lights of unfamiliar colors formed into floating rings in the air, hovering around them. This vivid experience was better than any fireworks display they had ever seen, and it was all around Abba. All sounds, light and even the air itself seemed to be alive and somehow shining for Him. The children began to understand that Abba was all power, and the One whom they had come from. He was love and the source of everything good.

Each moment in the lap of their Father felt like forever. He looked so young and also so old at the same time, and all of them could see resemblances to their own dad and mom in Him. It was impossible not to stare. As He was enjoying the sounds and songs around Him, the children stared at His radiant skin, His flowing white hair and especially His eyes—eyes that held within them all of the oceans and seas, all of the stars in the sky. His eyes could see all that could ever be seen and all that has ever existed.

Missy stared at His large, strong hands that held her from falling off of His lap. His hands surged with strength, making her feel loved and safe.

Time was not a thought in this place—just joy, loud worship, zipping lights and throngs of praises echoing in every direction.

As the songs kept on, Abba made it so they could hear Him amidst the noise, and He talked to each of them personally, encouraging them and revealing portions of their purpose. He spoke to them of adventures they would discover, people in Dulu that they would help, and battles with the Liar that they would win. For Aisha specifically, He mentioned a group of people that she would lead and another tribe that she would help called the Taris-Ketures.

For all of the children, He promised that He would go with them by His Sacred Breath. He said that the Breath which they could feel on their faces as He spoke to them would soon be in them, leading and comforting them along the way. He told them that there were many adventures ahead, and they would soon experience the ride of their lives.

After what seemed like years, the children felt a change coming. In a moment they found themselves once again on the high mountain pass, the songs, sounds and lightning gone. They stood outside of the gates of Thanks on a mountain ridge overlooking Dulu in the distance far below.

Kaboo slowly sat on the ground and then fell onto his back, with his arms outstretched and out of breath, as if he has just completed a race. It felt like they had traveled from a distant planet up in space and had just returned and landed back on earth. Lucas fell to his knees, trying to grasp some of what had just happened. The girls let out whimpering sounds mixed with giggles of joy as they rolled around on the ground. Rolly sat down with his eyes closed, unable to speak. Words and years, new sights and old understandings with purpose and delight had flooded their bodies.

Their clothes were glowing like the Shining Man's were, and their eyes were full of light and life. They each had changed hearts and were free from every fear and worry. After several minutes, the children began to recover from their experience, and they began looking around at the beautiful mountain and the grass they were sitting on. Everything on the mountain seemed dull and quiet compared to the place they had just been and the sights they had just experienced.

Down far below them was Dulu, looking completely dark, lifeless and uninviting. Going back to Dulu was like going into a prison compared to where they had been. Yet somehow, and for some strange reason, the children felt the love of Abba for Dulu inside of them, and they wanted to help those living under the dark cloud in the dry sand below.

Aisha remembered the words the Rock had spoken to her in the beginning and began to speak to the others.

"When I first found the Rock, here is what He said to me: 'I came down from the Ancient One to help you; now you must climb down from Me to help them.'" She looked around at her five friends and said, "Abba wants us to go back to Dulu to help them."

"You are right," said Kaboo. "Let's help Dulu!" he shouted, and Rolly and Isabelle agreed.

"I want to help my parents, too," said Missy. "I want to bring them here to meet Abba."

The children rose to their feet and started to walk down the mountain toward Dulu, all older in experience and younger with joy than they were at the beginning of the day. They knew that Abba wanted to help Dulu, and they were the help He was sending.

Chapter V
THE SLIDE

No path was visible on which to travel back through the forest below, and they found themselves in an unfamiliar place on the wonderful mountain. The same light that was in the room with Abba was still emanating from the children, making their faces shine. They all felt empowered like super heroes to live boldly without fear of failing or fear of others' opinions. Even more than that, they felt loved.

Kaboo decided to climb down from the rocks to find a way toward Dulu, and the rest followed. After walking only a short distance down through the rocks, the children heard the sound of trickling water at the top of a steep meadow. It wasn't a loud waterfall or a vast river, but it was the sound of a small creek. Kaboo ran several yards toward the sound, where a smattering of fir trees stood. There, bubbling out from the midst of numerous large stones, was clear water coming out of the side of the mountain. As the water reached the cool mountain air, vapors rolled off the top of the water, rising slowly until disappearing.

The water coming out of the side of the mountain collected in a small pool resembling a large bathtub, naturally hewn in stone, just before overflowing and running down through the mountain meadow. The water was crystal clear, and the rays of sun danced wildly through the water on the bottom of the pool, lighting up glistening rocks on the bottom.

Lucas and Rolly scrambled over the rocks and bent over to get a drink of the water as it bubbled to the surface. Kaboo excitedly shouted, "Come here guys, look at this!" Kaboo was several feet below the pool, watching the sparkling water wind down through the meadow.

Kaboo exclaimed, "This looks like a gigantic water slide! Look!" The children watched the waters quickly slip down the smooth stone that wound through the meadow and down into the trees below.

"Wow!" the kids said together with big eyes, trying to imagine such a ride compared to the small water slide at the Dulu swimming pool. At the same time, they felt a bit scared of something this dangerous. The kids followed the water slide with their eyes as it disappeared into the forest and the unknown path below them.

"I bet Abba put this here for us to slide down," Kaboo said as he approached the water, desperately wanting to give it a try. "This will be a blast!"

"Wait!" said Lucas. "We don't know if this is safe. We don't know what will happen once we pick up speed, and we don't know where the water might take us once we get down into those trees. What if someone gets hurt?"

For a moment, they all were quiet. Lucas was right. It was unknown and dangerous. Kaboo seemed impervious to considering anything but jumping in. He jumped back and forth over the stream like an excited dog ready to eat dinner, imagining how fun it would be to slide down the mountain.

Dulu

Kaboo said, "Come on you guys! This will be the ride of our lives. We'll be fine."

"Famous last words," Lucas quipped, a little sarcastically.

Then Aisha's eyes lit up as she glanced back up at the mountain and then back toward the others. "Hey you guys. Do you remember what Abba just said to us? He said that very soon we would have the ride of our lives." Aisha then looked straight at Isabelle for agreement. "Remember? I think this is what He was talking about. Kaboo is right."

Kaboo didn't wait another second. He sprung into the water on his rear and quickly began sliding down through the meadow and out of sight with a loud yell that echoed down the mountain and into the trees.

Hesitating for only a moment, Aisha jumped in next, followed by Rolly and Isabelle. Lucas was last, making sure that Missy got in first. He was still very unsure that this was a good idea.

The water slide was exhilarating. It dropped quickly with smooth bumps, jumps and turns down through the grass. The children, all yelling and screaming and bouncing, slid down the large

KABOO DIDN'T WAIT ANOTHER SECOND. HE SPRUNG INTO THE WATER ON HIS REAR AND QUICKLY BEGAN SLIDING DOWN THROUGH THE MEADOW AND OUT OF SIGHT

mountain, winding around the trunks of massive trees and through large mountain meadows.

At one point they passed through a herd of deer eating grass. The deer lifted their heads with grass hanging out of the sides of their mouths, frozen in place as six wild kids slid by them. Missy began waving at them saying, "Hello, Mr. Deer." As the children whizzed by, yelling in delight, the deer appeared to smile back at them.

The rushing water pushed them for what must have been a mile, moving them past another meadow and then narrowing and slowing for a moment before opening up into a large canyon that was carved into the mountain. The canyon was full of large, colorful trees on both sides. Among them were also smaller trees that crowded the bank of the flowing creek. The trees lined the canyon from top to bottom like a huge auditorium, and the slide wound its way down among the towering giants.

As Lucas entered the vast canyon on the slide, he could see the leaves on the trees begin to shake as the mercy winds breathed on them. The sun reflected off the moving leaves, causing the forest to glisten. Dozens of birds both large and small were soaring overhead, following the children down the mountain like watchers.

When Kaboo passed down through the canyon, yelling most of the way, the trees bent over from one side to another, watching him slide by. By the time Lucas and Missy approached, the limbs on all of the trees were smacking one another, making a thundering noise that echoed through the forest. The slide slowed down enough for the children to capture the moment, and the trees clearly looked happy and stared at them, clapping their limbs and branches together loudly as they passed by. The children realized in amazement that the trees were alive and cheering them down the mountain. Then all of the forest began clapping and swaying after the slippery riders slid past them, roaring a deafening sound of thunder that was unlike any noise they had heard. Thousands and thousands of living trees, oaks, pines, red woods, aspens, firs and cedars gave a thunderous applause to the six riders slipping past them.

Toward the bottom of the canyon, they saw the top of a gigantic tree. This tree, alone in the middle of the canyon, rose hundreds of feet into the air, and the slide was heading directly toward it. Kaboo braced for smacking right into it when suddenly the slide underneath him disappeared. He free-fell down about twenty feet over a waterfall until he made a cannon-ball splash into a pool of water that flowed around the base of the largest tree in Nifi.

Kaboo swam to the edge of the pool near the tree and stood up in the warm, shallow water. He slowly looked up at the tree, which was as wide as a wall. The tree was so tall that he fell over backward into the water trying to see its top.

Aisha, Rolly and the others came yelling over the waterfall into the bubbling waters behind Kaboo. Kaboo began laughing loudly at their contorted bodies and surprised faces as they rushed over the edge and into the pool.

A sound of cracking and screeching rumbled from the gigantic tree as it bent its top from high in the sky toward the children to see them. With a sudden movement, the massive limbs high over their heads came swooping together from east and west with a series of smacking sounds. The great clap from the tree echoed off the sides of the canyon, joining with the other clapping trees.

The Slide

The children, all together in the pool now, looked at one another in awe. Needles landed in their hair, and small cones fell to the water all around them from the clapping limbs above. They had never had such an audience before. Then the tree stopped clapping and raised his limbs a hundred feet in the air toward Nifi and began to stretch and jump up and down on the ground, as if dancing and celebrating. The reverberations from the tree shook the ground like an earthquake, sending a rumble through the ground that caused all of the other trees around to do the same. The entire forest erupted in celebration toward Nifi over these six tiny children who were standing waist-deep in a pool of water with smiles on their faces and tree needles in their hair.

The children were mesmerized by this display and the dust and noise that this celebration created. The children found the celebration contagious and started jumping up and down themselves, splashing in the water and joining with the trees in the party. The whole earth seemed to be celebrating something. It felt like they were back in the huge chambers of Abba and He was enjoying the dance.

After a few minutes, Kaboo noticed the cones and floating needles were moving to the end of the pool and flowing over it, continuing down the mountain. He motioned to the others to follow, and while the chorus of trees still clapped and jumped, the children jumped back onto the slide.

Beyond the gigantic tree, the slide became wider as other streams joined them. They rushed even faster down the mountain, screaming and yelling with excitement. At times they would slide very fast, and the children became scared. Then the slide would level out a bit, slowing down just enough to allow them to catch their breath before dropping once again like a dozen roller coasters in one.

The slide rounded a large turn to the right and then disappeared under the ground into darkness. Some of the children screamed out loud as they slid at top speed into the darkness inside of the earth. Lucas held onto Missy tightly as she slid in front of him and hoped this wasn't the danger he feared earlier.

The darkness continued, and the slide dropped even more steeply. It felt like they were going into the center of the earth. The slide slowed just a bit, and a dot of light appeared in the distance, helping quiet the screams and calm the fears. For a few moments, everything was silent. The light grew larger and larger while the water sloshed them through the pathway underground. Hanging roots were now visible just above their heads.

The children tried to brace for what might happen when they came out of the earth. They reached the opening and only the sky was seen as the children were shot out into the light and open air. They once again fell into a pool the size of a small lake. Plunging under water, all went silent other than bubbles and the waterfall pouring into the lake. Kaboo came up for air first with a burst of laughter that he could not contain, echoing around the pool of refreshing water. One by one, the remaining kids came flying down the slide and into the pool of water. Lucas had let go of Missy as they entered the air, and after re-emerging on the surface, he couldn't find her. He panicked internally for a moment until her little head popped up and a huge smiling face rose out of the fresh water. When they all surfaced, they joined Kaboo in raucous and uncontrollable laughter. They were safe and dizzyingly happy.

Laughing and trying to swim toward the shore was the difficult part. They sucked in a bit of water, coughed, and giggled some more. After they reached the shoreline, they continued splashing one another with soaking wet clothes and matted hair.

As the children finally stopped splashing and got out of the lake, they thanked Abba for such a fun slide. Then a strong and powerful wind roared down the slide and over their heads, swirling around their bodies. The wind was warm and fresh but strong against their faces, blowing their hair all around and drying them quickly. It reminded them of the mercy winds, but it was much stronger, like a harmless tornado encircling each of them. As the winds twisted around them, they could again hear singing, making them feel warm with the presence of Abba. Then, while the winds wrapped around them like a blanket, deep inside the children—from their stomachs—began to arise sounds and noises that they had never before spoken.

Strange and unknown words leaked through their lips. It was as if they were from another world and masters of another language. Each child, beginning with little Rolly, spoke unusual yet beautiful words. In wonder, the kids watched one another while new words formed in their mouths and then joined the winds. Joy, wonder and warmth filled them while they spoke in their own unique language, and it was as if they were talking to Abba in a secret code that only He knew. Soon, some of the kids began laughing. Missy laughed so hard at the funny tones coming from her brother, Lucas, that she couldn't stand on her feet anymore.

Some of their speech sounded eastern, and some sounded like an ancient native dialect, while others spoke in a more guttural-sounding foreign speech. Speaking loudly and sometimes softly in these languages, having no idea what they were saying, the six kids from the land of sand had a blast talking in the midst of the winds.

Lucas managed to speak in his own language, saying loudly to everyone, "What are we saying?" with a large smile and a laugh.

"I don't know, but you sure sound funny," Missy responded, enjoying another laugh at her brother.

"I feel like we are bragging on the greatness of Abba," responded Isabelle. We just don't know what we are saying exactly."

"I don't know what I'm saying," said Kaboo, "but this is awesome. The winds are giving us these words."

In the midst of laughter and speaking jibberish-sounding words, the kids began walking toward Dulu, switching back and forth from English to their new language along the way.

Each one recounted stories of the events of the day as they headed toward Dulu—the experience with Abba, the death-defying slide down the mountain and the strange languages. Kaboo had just finished his version of the trip down the slide when they all suddenly realized they had passed over from the beautiful land back into Dulu. They looked at one another in silence and turned around to see the pit that was behind them, but they didn't remember walking over it. The pit was of no concern or dread when coming from Nifi; it was as if it didn't exist at all. Only from Dulu did it look ominous. It was then that Missy noticed that their clothes were already dry and that they were walking on sand again.

"Look, our clothes are dry," she said. "The winds must have dried them, but how did we get across the pit?"

No one could figure out what had happened or how they got to where they were.

Rolly mentioned that he was hungry, and they all realized they had not eaten anything since breakfast. Everyone else suddenly felt hungry as well. Lucas looked at his watch and exclaimed, "This can't be!"

"What?" asked Isabelle, "What time is it?"

"It should be dinner time by now, but my watch still says 10:10 am! The water must have ruined my watch," Lucas said as he shook it and held it to his ear, doubting the time it projected.

"That's the same time it was when we were going up the mountain," said Rolly. "The water didn't break it."

Lucas looked up into the sky, shading his eyes from the sun with his hand, noticing that it hadn't moved. "I don't get it," he said. "Maybe it's been three days since we left, and we just don't know it."

"It will be okay," Aisha confidently stated.

A bit shyly, Isabelle said, "Hey guys. I think we are supposed to do something."

"What is it?" said Lucas.

"I think Abba wants us to go to one of the cottages on Bell Road, just up ahead," Isabelle said hesitantly.

"How do you know that?" asked Aisha.

"Because I just saw a picture in my mind of a big bell that had a drawing of a door on the side of it with the number 119. And then, as I was thinking about it, I remembered that Bell Road was just ahead of us. I know it's weird," said Isabelle, looking around to see if they thought she was crazy.

"After all that has just happened, nothing is weird anymore," Aisha stated, to everyone's amusement.

"Let's do it and see what happens," said Kaboo adventurously. "Maybe they have some food," he quipped with a smile.

The group decided to head for the cottages on Bell Road, which were on the far outskirts of Dulu. In a few minutes, they found a door that actually had the number 119 on it. Turning to see the smile on Isabelle's face, Aisha stepped toward the door and extended her hand to knock.

Chapter Six

NAHBI'

Knock, knock, knock.

The kids were very quiet, and Aisha heard some stirring inside as she stepped back from the door. It took awhile for the person to open up. Then two locks were unlatched, and the door slowly opened, revealing a very old man with bright blue eyes and a friendly smile.

"Well hello, friends," the thin old man said. "Please come in so I can help you today."

They all looked at one another a bit curiously, and then Isabelle led the way through the door. They smelled food cooking on the stove, and their hunger grew even more, but they remained quiet.

Inside of this tiny cottage was a couch, one chair and an end table that had a lamp on it. In between the couch and chair was a small coffee table with books and papers scattered all around. The old man asked them to sit down and make themselves comfortable as he walked over and sat down in his chair. The children sat on the couch and the floor, staring at his warm blue eyes, feeling very safe in this place—like they were at a grandpa's home.

"I've been waiting for you to arrive for some time, little ones," he said, though treating them as friends and not children. "Tell me your names," he said as he lovingly looked at Isabelle, who sat down first.

Isabelle told him her name, and the rest of the kids followed. The old man pondered a little bit and looked at each one of them for a moment, silently and a little awkwardly.

"What is your name, and how old are you?" Missy boldly asked. Lucas quickly gave her a little nudge on the arm as if to say that wasn't an appropriate question.

With a smile, the old man said, "Nahbi. Nahbi is what I'm called...but when I was young like you, I was called Josiah Williams. I'm eighty-seven years

"I'VE BEEN WAITING FOR YOU TO ARRIVE FOR SOME TIME, LITTLE ONES," HE
SAID, THOUGH TREATING THEM AS FRIENDS AND NOT CHILDREN.

young." Nahbi continued, not at all embarrassed to admit his age, while touching his chest with his hand, "Abba has taken care of me all of this time." When he mentioned Abba, he said His name like he really knew Him, and it was the first time they had ever heard an adult call the Ancient One *Abba*. They were thrilled that the old man knew the same Father they knew.

Nahbi then reached out for a round tin of cookies on the coffee table in front of him and handed it to Isabelle. She took two and passed the tin around the room for the others. The kids quickly scarfed down two or three cookies each, wishing they could have about ten more.

"I see that you are quite hungry, huh?" said Nahbi. "Let me see what we have for lunch." He slowly got up from his chair and shuffled into his small kitchen only a few feet away. On the stove was a small pan of chili that he had made.

"I've already eaten, but let me fix you up a bowl," he said to the pleasure of everyone. Kaboo was thinking he could eat five bowls all by himself, but he couldn't imagine that there would even be enough for two of them to eat.

NAHBI'

"I didn't make a lot, but I'm sure it will be enough," Nahbi said.

To their great surprise, Nahbi scooped six large bowls of chili out of his small pan, distributing them to the children, and they all ate their fill of chili and bread. After they finished, Nahbi began telling them that the Ancient One had shown him that six awakened kids would come to his home one day, and he was to give them special gifts when they came.

"I've been preparing for you to come, getting your gifts ready for a couple of years now," Nahbi said. The kids all looked at one another, amazed at these words.

He leaned over and pulled several books out from underneath the papers on his coffee table and began handing them out to each of them, connecting eyes with each child as he transferred the book with a smile. All of the children felt that they had just received something extremely valuable and full of power, though they weren't quite sure what had just been placed in their hands.

"What you now hold in your hands is alive," Nahbi began as the kids stared at the books. Each book was wrapped in faded blue covers with no words on the outside and seemed quite old.

Nahbi continued, "Things that appear old and boring can often be some of the most treasured and wonderful things in the world," he said as he turned to the end table next to him and picked up his own copy of the same book. Nahbi's copy was very worn out, the corners frayed and curled with use. The old man held his book as though it were his most prized possession. Grasping the worn book with both hands, Nahbi said, "Many people have died to preserve this book for you. They were chased down and killed by agents of the Liar because the Liar doesn't want you to read and eat these words. He hates it when you read and believe the words inside. When you read the words in your book, the haze of lies fades away around you because it is truth. You will see and think clearly."

"The words in this book are not only living, capable of disintegrating the haze, but the words are also food for the person inside of your skin— the person who you really are," he said intently. The children listened carefully to this old man who seemed to know all of the special secrets and mysteries. Lucas and Aisha began flipping through some of the pages of the book as he spoke, wondering how black-and-white words could be alive.

"The words inside tell the story of the love that the Ancient One has for you and all that He has done for you, even before you were born. As you read with your eyes, eat the words with your hearts, not just your brains, and swallow them to your toes. Just as you ate my cookies, allow your hearts to consume and believe the words of this book. You will find them tasty and sweet," he said. "Do you understand?" Nahbi asked, and each of them nodded. He seemed to be a man who had eaten a lot of the book himself. "This book is a love letter, written and preserved for you," he continued. "The words will taste like honey on your inside and will help you understand how much you are loved. And they will light the path of your journey, showing you how to treat others. Most importantly," Nahbi gestured with his hand, "the words are meant to remind you to always talk to the Great Shepherd and Abba, who are with you always."

A hunger to begin reading the love letter from the Ancient One filled the hearts of the children and made them wonder how it tasted like honey.

"I almost forgot," Nahbi then said. "Let me show you something else that the book will do for you." The old man held his book and, concentrating, focused somewhere beyond the ceiling in his tiny home. The book suddenly became a large shining sword in his hands, glistening with light, razor-sharp.

The children's jaws dropped open, and Missy gasped. Kaboo jumped to his feet with excitement, his book in hand, as he watched Nahbi hold his huge, sharp sword.

"This book reveals the words from the Ancient One that disintegrate the haze and cut through darkness," Nahbi shared while holding the sword that was lighting up the room even more. "When you feel depressed or anxious, when you feel discouraged or attacked by the Liar's haze, the words inside of this book and in your heart will become like a sword that will chase away depression and anxiety," Nahbi said and then paused as the sword quickly transformed back into the dull-looking book in his hands. He looked back at the children and said, "The more that you eat the words of this book, the larger and sharper your own sword will become, and it will help you and others."

"This book will also teach you about the Sacred Breath, and the Sacred Breath will explain the Ancient Treasure and the Great Mystery to you. You will all find power coming out of you when you believe and share these words with others," Nahbi said then stopped, as if he had told them too many things for them to take in at the moment.

Nahbi turned and slowly set his book back on the table as if nothing extraordinary had just taken place. He asked, "Do you remember the words that were written on the bridge over the pit and the words that were on the Way that led up to the Ancient One?" Without waiting for their answer, he continued, "Those words are the same as those written down in these old books."

"You've been across the bridge?" asked Missy. "And walked up Nifi?" she added.

"Why, yes, I have, sweetie," Nahbi answered with a grin and glimmer in his eye. "Every day," he said matter-of-factly to her, as if he were a child who had just been there with them.

The children were amazed that Nahbi knew about the bridge, the Way and so much about the Abba. Nahbi then told them that they had much to do and learn in the next few days and that others like himself would help them. With that, Nahbi used his arms to push up out of his chair, standing slowly to his feet. He slowly walked over to a tall wooden cabinet next to his kitchen.

"There are even more things that I am supposed to give you," said Nahbi as he opened the double doors. Hanging in the cabinet were six silver breastplates with belts, helmets, boots and glowing shields.

"Cooool!" shouted the three boys as they saw Nahbi remove a shining helmet from the cabinet.

The children rose to their feet, and Nahbi began handing each of them armor engraved with a special name on the helmets. The names were all unique, but the children didn't understand what they meant.

"Each of you has a name that your parents gave you, and each of you has a special name that Abba has given to you," Nahbi explained as he handed out the armor. "One day Abba will reveal your new name to you, but it is engraved on your helmet for now to remind you that you have purpose in this life and in the life with Him beyond this one."

All of this armor was light yet strong, fitting each one of them perfectly. Nahbi told them that they had a great mission ahead and that the Liar would shoot flaming missiles at them, but none of his weapons could penetrate their armor as long as they wore it everyday.

"Won't we look a little strange to everyone in Dulu as we wear this armor?" asked Isabelle, looking at the other kids in their armor.

"No," said Nahbi. "The armor is invisible to everyone but you and those who know Abba. As soon as you walk out of this door, no one will know that you are wearing it, and you will hardly feel it yourselves." He paused, wanting to make sure the children understood the importance of his words. "But it is important that you put it on each and every day so that you will not be hurt by the Liar.

As he said this, the kids became aware that Nahbi himself was wearing similar—but less shiny—armor.

"He especially will come against your mind with thoughts of doubt and accusation and fear, so keep your helmet on at all times," said Nahbi as he held up Rolly's helmet, admiring it and then tapping it on the side as if to make sure it was strong.

"Oh, I need to tell you how your armor will grow even stronger than it is now," he excitedly said. Your armor grows stronger and your sword gets sharper as you eat and believe the words of the ancient book that I gave each of you, and as you talk with Abba." As he said these words, Lucas saw a light flash from Nahbi's eyes. Nahbi continued, and Lucas looked around to see if anyone else had seen the flash of light. "Talk with Abba about everything in your lives, and ask Him all of your questions," he said and then paused. "He always answers."

Nahbi tightened the breastplate straps around Kaboo and continued, "The ancient book and the Sacred Breath will also tell you about all of your armor and show you how to use it. Each piece of your armor will protect you and help others. You may need to help one another put the armor on. You'll need to stick together no matter what happens, and make sure that you always love each other. The Liar is mean and vicious, and he'll try to separate you and give you reasons not to wear your armor, but he is no match for the Sacred Breath that lives inside of you and the love you have for one another."

NAHBI'

At that moment, Isabelle asked, "What are we are supposed to do in Dulu with this armor? The eagle and Abba said we were on a mission, but we aren't quite sure what we'll do."

"The Sacred Breath will lead you, and the book I gave you will guide you and show you the amazing things He has for you," Nahbi said with a smile. "There is nothing to worry about or fear. He'll show you what to do, and the love inside will compel you."

"What is the Sacred Breath?" questioned Lucas.

"The Sacred Breath is the invisible Abba living inside of you. As you breathe, He breathes in you; as you think, He is connected to your thoughts. As you do what He says, you will find Him doing miraculous things through you," Nahbi said with an intensity in his voice.

"Abba lives inside of us?" asked Rolly, looking around at the others, trying to imagine how in the world the huge Abba could fit inside of himself or little Missy.

Looking at Rolly, who was again sitting on the floor, Nahbi said, "Oh, yes. The Sacred Breath came to Dulu soon after the Rock came out of the pit. Abba wants to be so close to you that He has found a way to be nearer to you than anyone or anything else—even closer to you than your parents. The Sacred Breath can do anything! He is able to fill the smallest person or the largest. He found a way to live inside of your body so that He can love you, have fun with you and lead you to help others." He handed Kaboo his shield as he said, "You will get to know Him each day, and your ears will hear Him speak if you listen and believe."

Nahbi then looked at Isabelle and answered her earlier question: "Yes, there is much more to learn, and you will. But more important than learning is helping others with what you already have. As you leave here and give away what you already have, the Sacred Breath will teach you more. He is the moving Spirit, and He instructs while you are doing things with Him."

"But what kinds of things are we supposed to do, and how do we start to help people?" asked Lucas.

Nahbi looked at all of them in the eyes and smiled. He said, "Remember when you were at the healing pool on the mountain? What did you see each other doing?"

NAHBI'

"How did you know about that?" asked Aisha.

"I saw you there, and some of your missions came to you there," Nahbi exclaimed.

"Like the blind seeing and arms growing out?" Isabelle questioned with amazement.

"Yes. Everything that you saw in Nifi, you can do in Dulu. Everything you dreamed of doing in Nifi, you can do in Dulu. Nothing is impossible," said Nahbi.

Chill bumps went up Aisha's arms and neck when he said that, and all of the kids were amazed that they were going to get to help people in this way. "Wow!" Kaboo shouted. "That is *awesome*. This is going to be even more fun than sliding down Nifi!"

"I don't know about that," said Missy, and everyone laughed.

The kids began imagining what might happen, and they felt such a closeness to Nahbi in this short time.

"We'd better get going guys," Lucas said, and he stood up again, looking at the others. "Thank you, Nahbi, for the food, the armor and all that you have told us...."

"Can we come back soon and visit?" Missy interrupted.

"Sure you can," he said, glancing down at Missy, who quickly threw herself toward him and gave him a big hug. All of the kids followed, thanked him and hugged him, which he seemed to enjoy.

"Don't forget the books I gave you," said Nahbi.

Walking out the door, with the sun high in the sky, the kids began running home, and Nahbi watched them disappear down the street from his door.

On the way home from Nahbi's cottage, the kids discussed how they would meet at Kaboo's fort on Sunday morning (the next day) and plan their next adventure. After Aisha told them how her parents weren't that excited about the Rock, they decided not to give all of the details of their adventure to their parents, especially since it seemed so unreal and their parents hadn't become awakened yet.

They decided to only tell them some things about Nahbi, and maybe a little about Abba. The kids didn't feel that their parents would be ready to hear about their journey over the pit and the land of Nifi quite yet. Although it would be very difficult not to tell their parents about every adventure they had today, they could feel the Sacred Breath inside of them, encouraging them to be loving to their parents and to listen to them, while treasuring every adventure from the day in their hearts.

The group hugged one another and gave high fives, laughing and so joyful they could hardly stand it. They didn't want to leave each other, and it seemed like they had just spent a year together in a foreign country. Their time together had changed each of them; it created in them a different love and friendship than they had ever experienced.

When they reached their homes, unbelievably, it was only about two in the afternoon on Saturday. It was nearly impossible not to share about Drenjee, the giant eagle, the slide, and, of course, Abba with their parents. Instead, the kids started asking their parents questions about the land of Nifi, the pit and what they knew about the Ancient One.

Most of the answers from the parents were vague, as if the land of Nifi and the Ancient One were an old fairy tale about a distant land. Nifi wasn't very real to them, and they certainly didn't speak with Him. Even though Nifi was clearly seen from Dulu, the cloud of lies over Dulu had made Nifi seem unreal and twisted, mean, distant and unreachable. This made them feel a little sad because their parents didn't yet know Abba. But they knew they would soon.

Although she was very tired, after going to bed, Aisha pulled out the book that Nahbi had given to her and opened it under the light of the lamp next to her bed.

The first thing she read was this:

"Believe me when I say that I am in Abba and Abba is in me; or at least believe on the evidence of the miracles themselves. I tell you the truth, anyone who has faith in me will do what I have been doing. They will do even greater things than these, because I am going to Abba. And I will do whatever you ask in my name, so that the Son may bring glory to the Father. You may ask me for anything in my name, and I will do it."

Reading this was like hearing everything they had experienced through the day: believing in the Rock, seeing the miracle of the Door and the bridge over the pit into Nifi, speaking with Abba, receiving armor and an ancient book from Nahbi. Aisha knew that the Son talked about in the book was the Rock she now knew personally. The book was telling her that she and anyone who believed could do powerful things. "Anyone" meant even kids like her.

Aisha, rolling over on her back and smiling, glanced out of the window and whispered, "Thank uou, Abba." In only a few seconds, Aisha fell into dream world.

Chapter Seven
LUTRU

Once again, the sun shone through Aisha's window, waking her up. It was Sunday morning, and Aisha awoke convinced that she had just had the most amazing dream of all time, full of large swimming fish, flying lions and mountain water slides. She was convinced it was a dream until she looked down and saw the book that Nahbi had given her intermingled with her covers. She grabbed it quickly, took a deep breath and closed her eyes, holding the book to her chest. *It wasn't just a dream*, she thought to herself. *It was real.* She reminisced about the encounter she had at the top of the Ancient One with Abba the day before. She looked out the window and there was Nifi. Aisha was overwhelmed at the thought that she had actually been there at the top of the mountain. The realization that she had been where so few have ever been, seen what so few have ever seen, began to sink in.

Her clock read 9:08 am. "I've got to get ready," Aisha said to herself, rushing toward her dresser and slinging a drawer open to grab some clothes quickly. After putting her shirt on, Aisha saw a quick sparkle in the air above her dresser. It caught her attention, and she looked that way. Suddenly, she realized that her helmet was perched on top of her dresser, waiting for her to put it on. It had seemed invisible until she saw the sparkle, and now it was clearly visible. She put both hands on the sides of the helmet and slipped it on over her head of dark hair. She looked around for the rest of the armor, thinking about Nahbi and his words to them. As she put each piece on, she realized that all of the armor was hardly noticeable, even to the wearer. She could barely feel it on her, but when she looked into her mirror, she could see it. She thought about her hair and reached up to touch it, and her fingers felt her thick hair. Then she thought about the helmet and could suddenly feel the helmet. It seemed that whatever she focused on, she could feel. Aisha crossed her right hand over her body toward the shield on her left hand. She could feel the edge of the shield with her right hand. But if she focused on just her left hand, the shield seemed to disappear.

Downstairs at breakfast, Aisha poured a bowl of Munchy-Crunch, the sweet cereal her mom let her have only on Sundays.

"Hey, honey," her mom said. "Why don't you slow down. What's the hurry this morning?" she said as Aisha slurped the cereal into her mouth like she was racing someone.

"Ish jush thaa I'm plannin' to meet my friens again at Kaboo's housh," Aisha replied with a mouth full of food, milk dripping out of the corner of her lips back into the bowl.

"Oh," her mom said with a grin, looking up at her while cutting up onions on the counter. "You remember that we were going to the fair this afternoon, don't you?" she asked, looking back down at the cutting board.

"Mmm....oh, yeah," said Aisha. "I forgot."

"You forgot?" asked her mom. "That surprises me, since you love the fair."

"Well," replied Aisha, swallowing a mouth full. "It's just that I've had so much fun with my friends that I forgot. But the fair sounds nice. What time are we going?"

"Let's leave here at five, and we can get some hot dogs and fresh corn on the cob for dinner at the fair," her mom said.

"Ok, Mom," she said kindly. "Can I go now if I'll be back before five?" Aisha asked. Compared to her experience yesterday, going to the fair was like having to clean the bathroom.

"As long as Kaboo's mom is okay with you being over there," she said, still a bit curious as to what could be more fun for Aisha than the fair. "Rolly will be there too, right?" her mom asked.

"Yep. Bye, Mom….love you," Aisha said as the door swung shut behind her and she ran through the sand.

Kaboo lived only about two blocks away. When Aisha arrived, Isabelle and Rolly were already there, way up in the tree fort that Kaboo had in his back yard. Aisha climbed the many steps that wrapped around the tree to get to the first level and then up the next several steps to the top level where they always met. The tree fort was the best and highest in the neighborhood, with a fun zip line that allowed the kids fly back to the ground.

Kaboo said that Lucas and Missy couldn't come until a little later, after they did some chores around the house. He also seemed very quiet and calm for Kaboo, especially after yesterday's adventure.

"Did all of that really happen yesterday?" asked Kaboo, seeming sad and doubtful for some reason.

"Of course it did," Aisha piped up quickly. "What happened yesterday was more real than anything we've ever done!" she said confidently. "Did you put your helmet on today, Kaboo?" she asked while looking at Rolly, too.

"No," replied Kaboo in a downtrodden tone. He looked up and could see a glimmer from the armor that the other three were wearing.

"Remember what Nahbi told us?" Isabelle said with fervor. "Doubt and lies are in the air over Dulu every day," she said. Aisha's shield seemed to appear brightly in her hand.

"Put your helmet on quickly," Isabelle directed Kaboo. "Your mind is getting hit by lies." As she said that, it was almost as if they could see a dark cloud swirling around Kaboo's head like a swarm of flies, lying to him.

Kaboo was still sluggish, unsure that what his friends were saying was true. "Huh," he grunted with his head low, staring at the floor of his tree fort.

Rolly suddenly got up, stepped into the harness on the zip line and jumped off the side of the fort. He bounced up and down a bit as he sailed through air, hanging from the line all the way down to the ground. He then quickly unharnessed himself and ran into Kaboo's house without a word. Moments later, Rolly returned with his arms full of Kaboo's shining armor—boots and all. Isabelle and Aisha climbed down the fort and helped Rolly carry it up. Just seeing the shield seemed to brighten Kaboo's countenance.

Aisha took Kaboo's helmet and plopped it over his curly dark hair while Isabelle helped put his breastplate on. In a moment, Kaboo came back to life, and his mind began thinking clearly again. He

THE TREE FORT WAS THE BEST AND HIGHEST IN THE NEIGHBORHOOD, WITH A FUN
ZIP LINE THAT ALLOWED THE KIDS FLY BACK TO THE GROUND.

155

looked up and smiled at them, and then he let out a growl as if to say, "I'm back."

"We can never forget our armor here in Dulu, even for one day," Isabelle said in a very serious tone, looking at all of the kids. "It's too dangerous to live without the armor that we've been given."

Aisha pulled out her ancient book from her book bag and opened it to the place she had read the night before. She read the words out loud:

Believe me when I say that I am in Abba and Abba is in me; or at least believe on the evidence of the miracles themselves. I tell you the truth, anyone who has faith in me will do what I have been doing. They will do even greater things than these, because I am going to Abba. And I will do whatever you ask in my name, so that the Son may bring glory to the Father. You may ask me for anything in my name, and I will do it.

Aisha then said, "I think this means that kids can do stuff that Abba's Son, the Good Shepherd, can do. Nahbi said that, too."

"So, what do we do?" asked Kaboo, now back into his adventurous spirit.

Everyone was silent for a few moments, and then Rolly began to talk.

"There are all of those older people down next to the Center Circle who beg for money. Some of them can't walk very well," Rolly said while looking at the others with compassion in his eyes. "I wonder if we should go there? When Kaboo asked what we should do, I began thinking about the old people there, and I imagined us making them smile," he added.

"But they smell bad," Kaboo said, wrinkling up his nose. The girls giggled at the look on his face.

Just then, Lucas and Missy came running into the yard out of breath, certainly having run all the way from their house. "Hey guys," Lucas said after reaching the top, and Missy managed a quick hello a few moments later.

Isabelle brought Lucas and Missy up to speed with what they were thinking about doing, and Missy said, "I was thinking this morning about giving some food away. We have a whole box of apples that we could give them."

"Good idea, Missy," said Isabelle. "Let's all go home, find something that we have to give away and meet at the Center Circle."

"Okay," Aisha responded, standing to her feet. All six kids jumped up, and each rode the zip line through the air and down to the ground and then scattered home.

A little while later, they met across the street from the Center Circle, where a dozen older men and a few women were lying around on the ground with dirty clothes and old bags around them.

All of the kids pulled out some of their gifts, which included apples, a hair comb, some fresh cornbread, a few cookies and even a chain necklace that Missy brought.

They gathered together for a moment in a circle, not quite sure what to do next. Lucas took a deep breath and looked toward Nifi, as if looking for guidance. He said, "Sacred Breath, help us love these people and do the things the Great Shepherd would do."

A little shyly, and somewhat nervously, the kids walked up to the people and began saying hello and handing out the things they had brought with them with a smile. Some of the people looked mean, and some others were very thankful. Isabelle suddenly felt the palms of her hands get very warm and slick. She stared at them and stopped for a second just before speaking to one of the men, who was sitting quietly in ragged clothing.

Isabelle looked down at the man and said, "Hello, sir...can I give you something?" The man slowly moved his head up toward her without saying anything. His eyes were completely white. "Uhh," Isabelle stumbled with her words for a moment, very surprised at what she was seeing. She breathed in louder than she meant to, a little unprepared. She remembered Lucas telling her about a man with white eyes at the healing pool on Nifi, and she glanced down again at her oily hands. She felt a confidence grow inside of her.

The man still hadn't spoken, and he expected her to be afraid and walk away like so many had before. Instead, Isabelle knelt down beside him and touched his hand. "Sir," she began, "I have some cookies for you. Will you take some?" she asked while gently placing one in his hand. He mumbled under his breath and then began smelling the cookie carefully, making sure this was no trick.

Isabelle gathered all of the courage and boldness she could muster while the old blind man took a small nibble of the cookie. "Sir, my name is Isabelle. I know that this may seem strange, but can I touch your eyes? I believe that you will see again."

The man still didn't say anything, but after an awkward few moments, he nodded his head ever so slightly just before taking another slow nibble of the cookie. Isabelle glanced over at Aisha, who was watching what was happening, as if to ask her to come and help. Aisha came near and got on her knees next to the man quietly also. Then she looked at Isabelle with kind eyes as if to say, "Go ahead. You can do it."

Isabelle very gently placed the palms of her hands over the closed eyelids of the old man. Quietly she said, "Eyes that cannot see, be healed by the power of the Good Shepherd and His Sacred Breath that lives inside of me."

She closed her eyes for a moment as she felt such a deep love and compassion for this old man she did not know. As she remembered the word of Lucas, a tear escaped her shut eyes and flowed down her cheek. She didn't feel anything but love for the man.

After several more seconds, she slowly pulled her hands away from the man. His eyes remained closed. Isabelle looked up at Aisha, who also had tears dripping down her cheeks. The other kids had come over and were kneeling around them quietly, watching and praying under their breath with her.

The man's eyelids began to quiver, and he slowly opened them, his face tilted toward the sky. As his lids opened, white eyes again appeared, to the disappointment of all the children. Then, moments later, as he looked up toward the sun, he suddenly made a noise. It was more of a groan, but then he made another sound. "I…" he stopped, while blinking rapidly. "I see." He stopped again, struggling to get the words out. A grayish color came over his eyes, followed by small black spots that began to appear in the center of each eye. Waves of emotion fell upon all of the kids as the man started making other noises. His frail hands starting quivering, and his body began shaking.

He dropped the half-eaten cookie into his lap and turned toward Isabelle, locked eyes with hers, and placed his frail hands on her arms. The gray then turned blue. He was seeing a person for the first time in his life.

The man fell into the arms of Isabelle as five kids began jumping up and down like the forest of trees, shouting and crying in celebration of the greatest thing they had ever witnessed.

The commotion caused the other people around the Circle to push toward the blind man to see what was happening. Soon they were all getting prayed for by the rest of the kids, whose faith was now surging.

When Rolly prayed for one of the older woman's knees, she suddenly felt a heat burning inside of her knee, and the pain disappeared. The noise from the children and the homeless people poured out through the street, and others from around the area began walking over to see what was going on. To their amazement, six children were touching and praying for lines of people who had gathered around them. Adults began shouting, some fainted and still others began crying themselves. The Sacred Breath put words into the children's mouths to pray and speak out for every person. The kids didn't even understand much of what they prayed.

THE MAN'S EYELIDS BEGAN TO QUIVER, AND HE SLOWLY OPENED
THEM, HIS FACE TILTED TOWARD THE SKY.

People of every age were feeling warmth in their bodies and joy in their hearts. Others were healed and freed from fears, pains and torments.

As the people gathered, Aisha felt compelled to climb up on the base of a flagpole that flew the Dulu flag in the center of the Circle. She climbed up onto the platform where the pole was mounted in the cement and stood on the base, hanging onto the pole with one hand.

She said, "Hello, people of Dulu. I have something to tell you." Her voice at first was soft, but it grew louder and more confident with every word. "The healing taking place is not being done by magic or by our power. What is happening is coming from Nifi!" When Aisha said Nifi, everyone turned and looked behind them toward the beautiful mountain in the distance, wondering how this could be.

Aisha continued, "Do you remember the Big Rock that we all saw in the sand just a few days ago?"

"Yes," muttered an older woman, frail yet listening to every word. "I remember hearing about it."

"Well, the Big Rock came from Nifi to help us. But some men didn't like it and threw the Big Rock into the Abyss. We saw the marks in the sand where they dragged Him. But it's okay; He is no longer there," she said, to their astonishment. "The Big Rock has come out of the Abyss and is back with Nifi. We saw Him ourselves."

"What?" questioned one of the men. "You saw it yourselves? What are you talking about? You kids are crazy! No one can go over to Nifi. It's impossible, and you are kids," he snarled with a disbelieving laugh.

Aisha looked at him kindly and said, "I think it's impossible for a blind man to see, too." At these words, the man stopped talking. Everyone looked at the man who was once blind but now seeing and smiling from ear to ear at Aisha. She continued with confidence, "The Big Rock *is* with Nifi, and He *is* real. He has sent us here to bring freedom and healing to all of Dulu by His Sacred Breath that lives inside of us. He loves you and is the one who is healing people here today."

Just then, an old woman began mocking them, laughing with a cackling laugh. She walked closer, her face furrowed with bitter wrinkles. "These children are false prophets," she uttered in a witchy voice. "They are rebellious little children who are tricking everyone," she said. "They are children who need to be punished and sent home."

The accusations felt evil and fearful, and they made Aisha feel wrong for standing up and speaking. Her stomach felt a pain after hearing these words. The woman then came close to Aisha, pointed at her and said, "You go home, little girl, and take your evil magic with you."

Aisha was shocked and a little scared at the same time. She had done nothing wrong, but the woman made her feel like she had. Aisha stopped talking and climbed down from the flagpole. Kaboo and Isabelle boldly stepped between the woman and Aisha. Isabelle looked up at her and said, "You are the one who needs to go home, lady."

The enraged woman turned to the crowd and continued to tell them not to listen to the children because they were rebellious and had evil magic.

The children had ever never experienced hatred and anger like this before, and made it Aisha want to go home. Aisha hugged the man who had received the miracle, and the children started walking back to Kaboo's house, while the enraged woman kept on muttering strange things, yelling with exaggerated gestures.

LUTRU

On the way back toward Kaboo's house, the kids were quiet. They felt very strange, and their joy had been stolen. About one block from Kaboo's home, they walked by an older man who was sitting on a bench at a bus stop. While they were passing by, he looked up and said, "Aisha." The children stopped, and, to their surprise, Nahbi was looking at them with a smile. The children greeted him like he was a grandfather they hadn't seen in awhile and ran to him.

Looking at Aisha, Nahbi said, "Wonderful things have happened in Dulu today."

Aisha looked down at the ground sadly.

"I saw light break through the dark cloud over Dulu today because of all of you," Nahbi said while holding an old cane made of twisted wood with both hands. "You have brought the land of Nifi to Dulu today. This is wonderful!" he exclaimed with a large smile.

The light in Aisha's eyes came back with Nahbi's words, and it was like she had just been given a cold cup of water on a very hot day.

"But an old woman, maybe even as old as you, came and yelled at us and told me I was evil," Aisha said to Nahbi.

"Did she really?" replied Nahbi with a serious look, pretending to be amazed.

"Yes," said all of the kids at once. "Yeah, she was a cranky old lady," added Kaboo.

"And I feel yucky, like I did something wrong," Aisha said sincerely, affected by the words that the woman had said.

"Well," said Nabhi, as he placed his left hand on his knee and leaned forward slightly. "How do you think Abba feels about you and what you have done today? Do you think He agrees with the cranky lady?"

"No," replied Lucas and the others.

"You are right," said Nahbi. "The Liar is the accuser, and he sometimes stirs up his slaves to say mean things to children of light to try and get them to stop giving love away. But don't worry or take their words to heart. Only allow what Abba says and thinks to affect you. And right now He is proud of you. You aren't evil; you are beautiful," Nahbi said with a bright and loving smile.

"Dulu has been waiting for you. Never let what others say or think—or the way that you feel—keep you from being love. The Sacred Breath is about to lead you into your next great adventure."

APPENDIX

Note from Author

Dear Reader:

The story you have just read is an allegory. In Greek, the word **Douloo** means "under bondage." This is where the land of "Dulu" is derived for the story. Dulu speaks of the bondage that the world was in before the Ancient of Days, or the "Ancient One," sent His Son, Jesus (the Rock, the Lamb, the Door, the Good Shepherd and the Way), to redeem (lutru) all of mankind.

The Dulu series describes how much God loves each person. It tells of how much He desires that we know His Son personally, that we hear and follow His voice into the adventure that He has for our lives with His Spirit (Sacred Breath) inside of us. Below this letter and on DuluKids.com are references to the Scriptures that provide the imagery and symbolism used in every chapter.

Through the years of your life, may each rock or grain of sand that you encounter be a reminder of the God who came down to be where you are. He is a God

Dulu

who is forever with you, thinking about you wherever you go, desiring to be your best friend, speaking and leading you into knowing Him and fulfilling your great purpose in Dulu.

In the adventure with you,

Matt

Appendix

Chapter One: The Rock

Dulu comes from the Greek word Douloo—meaning to enslave, under bondage. Dulu speaks of the land that is under bondage to the Liar before the Rock arrives and everything begins to change.

Kaboo was the real name for Samuel Morris (1873-1893), a boy from the Kru tribe in Liberia, Africa. Kaboo was kidnapped and cruelly treated until he had a supernatural experience with God that led him out of his captivity. Through a floating light in the jungle, Kaboo was led barefoot to freedom, where he met missionaries who led him to Christ. He then embarked upon a remarkable journey around the world to learn more about the Holy Spirit, and along the way, he changed the lives of thousands of people.

Scriptures from which the imagery and symbols were derived:

"I kept looking until thrones were set up, and the Ancient of Days took {His} seat;" Daniel 7:9

"It is of the LORD's mercies that we are not consumed, because his compassions fail not. They are new every morning: great is thy faithfulness." Lamentations 3:22-23

"To You, O Lord, I call; My rock, do not be deaf to me, Lest, if You be silent to me, I become like those who go down to the pit." Psalms 28:1

"Be to me a rock of habitation, to which I may continually come; You have given commandment to save me, for You are my rock and my fortress." Psalms 71:3

"The Rock! His work is perfect, for all His ways are just; a God of faithfulness and without injustice, Righteous and upright is He." Deuteronomy 32:4

"Trust in the LORD forever, for in GOD the LORD, we have an everlasting Rock." Isaiah 26:4

"...But the stone that struck the statue became a great mountain and filled the whole earth." Daniel 2:35

"...there was nothing beautiful or majestic about His appearance, nothing to attract us to Him." Isaiah 53:2 (Living)

"My sheep hear My voice, and I know them, and they follow Me; and I give eternal life to them, and they shall never perish; and no one shall snatch them out of My hand." John 10:27-28

"He must increase, but I must decrease." John 3:30

APPENDIX

Chapter Two: The Door

".... and lo, I am with you always, even to the end of the age." Matthew 28:20

"The angel said to the women, "Do not be afraid; for I know that you are looking for Jesus who has been crucified. He is not here, for He has risen, just as He said." Matthew 28:5-6

"Truly I say to you, unless you are converted and become like children, you will not enter the kingdom of heaven." Matthew 18:3

"I am the Door; if anyone enters through Me, he will be saved, and will go in and out and find pasture." John 10:9

"Truly I say to you, whoever does not receive the kingdom of God like a child will not enter it at all." Luke 18:17

"For the gate is small and the way is narrow that leads to life, and there are few who find it." Matthew 7:14

Dulu

Chapter Three: The Land of Nifi

"The LORD is my shepherd, I shall not want. He makes me lie down in green pastures; He leads me beside quiet waters. He restores my soul; He guides me in the paths of righteousness For His name's sake." Psalms 23:1-3

"I am the good shepherd, and I know My own and My own know Me," John 10:14

"I am the way, and the truth, and the life; no one comes to the Father, but through Me." John 14:6

"But He was pierced through for our transgressions, He was crushed for our iniquities; The chastening for our well-being fell upon Him, And by His scourging we are healed." Isaiah 53:5

"...and said, "Truly I say to you, unless you are converted and become like children, you will not enter the kingdom of heaven." Matthew 18:3

"But when Jesus saw this, He was indignant and said to them, "Permit the children to come to Me; do not hinder them; for the kingdom of God belongs to such as these." Mark 10:14

"The Spirit Himself testifies with our spirit that we are children of God," Romans 8:16

Appendix

"I have no greater joy than this, to hear of my children walking in the truth." 3 John 4

"He found him in a desert land, and in the howling waste of a wilderness; He encircled him, He cared for him, He guarded him as the pupil of His eye. Like an eagle that stirs up its nest, that hovers over its young, He spread His wings and caught them, He carried them on His pinions. The LORD alone guided him, And there was no foreign god with him. He made him ride on the high places of the earth.." Deuteronomy 32:10-13

"He will cover you with His pinions, and under His wings you may seek refuge; His faithfulness is a shield and bulwark." Psalms 91:4

"Enter into His gates with thanksgiving, His courts with praise." Psalms 100:4

"And the four living creatures, each one of them having six wings, are full of eyes around and within; and day and night they do not cease to say, "Holy, holy, holy is the Lord God, the Almighty, who was and who is and who is to come." Revelation 4:8

"Out from the throne come flashes of lightning and sounds and peals of thunder. And there were seven lamps of fire burning before the throne, which are the seven Spirits of God...." Revelation 4:5

Dulu

Chapter Four: The Ancient One

"Enter His gates with thanksgiving And His courts with praise. Give thanks to Him, bless His name." Psalms 100:4

"I will praise the name of God with song And magnify Him with thanksgiving." Psalms 69:30

"Jesus said to him, "I am the way, and the truth, and the life; no one comes to the Father but through Me." John 14:6

"Therefore let us draw near with confidence to the throne of grace, so that we may receive mercy and find grace to help in time of need." Hebrews 4:16

"The first creature was like a lion, and the second creature like a calf, and the third creature had a face like that of a man, and the fourth creature was like a flying eagle. And the four living creatures, each one of them having six wings, are full of eyes around and within; and day and night they do not cease to say, "Holy, holy, holy is the Lord God, the Almighty, who was and who is and who is to come." Revelation 4:7-8

"For you have not received a spirit of slavery leading to fear again, but you have received a spirit of adoption as sons by which we cry out, "Abba! Father!""

Appendix

The Spirit Himself testifies with our spirit that we are children of God," Romans 8:15-16

"Then I saw a great white throne and Him who sat upon it, from whose presence earth and heaven fled away, and no place was found for them." Revelation 20:11

Chapter Five: The Slide

"For you will go out with joy And be led forth with peace; The mountains and the hills will break forth into shouts of joy before you, And all the trees of the field will clap their hands." Isaiah 55:12

"And suddenly there came from heaven a noise like a violent rushing wind, and it filled the whole house where they were sitting... And they were all filled with the Holy Spirit and began to speak with other tongues, as the Spirit was giving them utterance... And when this sound occurred, the crowd came together, and were bewildered because each one of them was hearing them speak in his own language." Acts 2:2-6

"'Cretans and Arabs—we hear them in our own tongues speaking of the mighty deeds of God.' And they all continued in amazement and great perplexity, saying to one another, 'What does this mean?'" Acts 2:11

Appendix

Chapter Six: Nahbi

Nahbi' means "hidden of the Lord" or "Jehovah's protection." In the story he is the old man who is very close to Abba, with prophetic giftings and guidance for the kids. This character is modeled after Joe Williams (1901-1992), who was my best friend during my later teen years. Joe stirred my faith, shared the supernatural and helped me to pursue God in ways I hadn't previously.

"But the Helper, the Holy Spirit, whom the Father will send in My name, He will teach you all things, and bring to your remembrance all that I said to you." John 14:26

"Your words were found and I ate them, And Your words became for me a joy and the delight of my heart; For I have been called by Your name, O LORD God of hosts." Jeremiah 15:16

"How sweet are Your words to my taste! Yes, sweeter than honey to my mouth!" Psalms 119:103

"Therefore, take up the full armor of God, so that you will be able to resist in the evil day, and having done everything, to stand firm. Stand firm therefore, HAVING GIRDED YOUR LOINS WITH TRUTH, and HAVING PUT ON THE BREASTPLATE OF

RIGHTEOUSNESS, and having shod YOUR FEET WITH THE PREPARATION OF THE GOSPEL OF PEACE; in addition to all, taking up the shield of faith with which you will be able to extinguish all the flaming arrows of the evil one. And take THE HELMET OF SALVATION, and the sword of the Spirit, which is the word of God." Ephesians 6:13-17

"For the word of God is living and active and sharper than any two-edged sword—piercing right through to a separation of soul an spirit, joints and marrow, and able to judge the thoughts and intentions of the heart." Hebrews 4:12

"For nothing will be impossible with God." Luke 1:37

Appendix

Chapter Seven: Lutru

Lutru comes from the Greek word lutroo, meaning—to release, ransom and redeem. It is what Rolly speaks out over Dulu as a prophecy that the land will be loosed and freed from it's bondage.

"The Spirit of the Lord is upon Me, because He anointed Me to preach the gospel to the poor. He has sent Me to proclaim release to the captives, and recovery of sight to the blind, to set free those who are oppressed, to proclaim the favorable year of the Lord." Luke 4:18-19

"I tell you the truth, anyone who believes in me will do the same works I have done, and even greater works, because I am going to be with the Father. You can ask for anything in my name, and I will do it, so that the Son can bring glory to the Father. Yes, ask me for anything in my name, and I will do it!" John 14:12-14

"I was watching Satan fall from heaven like lightning. Behold, I have given you authority to tread on serpents and scorpions, and over all the power of the enemy, and nothing will injure you." Luke 10:18, 19

"You are the light of the world" Matthew 5:14

THANKS:

I'm very thankful for the time I had with two friends of Abba, Joe Williams and Bob Jones, who impacted my life profoundly. Thanks to my parents, Phil and Lynda Peterson, who first revealed the Ancient One to me and raised me on the mountain. Thanks to Wendy Dixon for the inspiration to keep moving toward publishing. Thanks to Sarah Roach, Dana Zondory, Lauren Olinger and Jacob Daniels for their efforts with the editing, layout, web-design and illustrations. Thanks to Aisha Šipilovi-Walth and Isabelle Lahaie for their generous gifts toward this story and the use of their own names for two of the characters in the book. Thanks to everyone else who gave toward this story.

Matt is the author of 'The Extraordinary Journey,' leads Awake Church (AwakeChurch. com), and is the founder of Hydrating Humanity (HydratingHumanity.org). He is a storyteller who loves history, the outdoors, adventure, and helping people find and live out their purpose. Matt resides in Winston-Salem, NC with his beautiful wife Debbie. Together they have five sons: Josiah, Seth, Sam, John and Andrew.

Jacob Daniels is a NC born artist whose art is focused on regional, spiritual, and humanitarian influences. His goal in art is to create thought-provoking imagery that is universally relatable, yet each viewer walks away with his or her own personal story. He lives in the mountains of Boone, NC with his wife Melina and son Lucca where they run their arts-based business Overflow Studios. (www. Overflowstudios.com)

FOR MORE INFORMATION OR TO ORDER PRINTS, VISIT DULUKIDS.COM

41367990R00106

Made in the USA
San Bernardino, CA
10 November 2016